Aloha
Summer

Bill Wallace

A MINSTREL®
BOOK

Published by POCKET BOOKS
New York   London   Toronto   Sydney   Singapore

A Minstrel Book published by
POCKET BOOKS, a division of Simon & Schuster Inc.
1230 Avenue of the Americas, New York, NY 10020

Copyright © 1997 by Bill Wallace

Published by arrangement with Holiday House, Inc.

ISBN: 0-671-02648-8

First Minstrel Books printing August 2000

10 9 8 7 6 5 4 3 2 1

A MINSTREL BOOK and colophon are registered trademarks of Simon & Schuster Inc.

Cover art by Frank Sofo

Printed in the U.S.A.

To
Kacey, Jon-Ed, and Kevin
from a world apart, yet a part of our world

Chapter 1

"Out of the frying pan, into the fire."

I never knew what that old-time saying Grandma used *really* meant—not until this very moment.

The wood rail felt cool against my cheek. The ocean spray was a fine mist, a fresh, gentle kiss on my forehead and neck.

Then the schooner rose from the trough and crested the next wave. White sails billowed and fluttered above my head. Once more the boat dropped to stir the ocean spray at the bow.

Only, when the schooner dropped, my stomach didn't. It—and everything in it—just kept going up. My death grip tightened on the rail. I leaned out a little. I threw up.

Sure enough—"Out of the frying pan, into the fire."

Man, I wished I was back home with Grandma. I could almost see her in her long skirt and apron. And, although she hadn't said anything as she waved good-bye to us at the Rock Island train station, I could see that look in her eye. The look that said:

"Y'all are jumping out of the frying pan, into the fire."

When I was little, I hadn't had any idea what that saying meant.

As I'd gotten older, I figured Grandma used the phrase mostly when talking about one of Daddy's "harebrained ideas." Fact was, it was Daddy's hare-brained ideas that got us into this mess to begin with.

Daddy was all the time tinkering with stuff. There was a big town about four miles east of our Oklahoma farm called Chickasha. There was probably might near three to four thousand people what lived there. Folks in Chickasha had indoor plumbing. None of the farmers did. So Daddy ran pipe from the cistern that caught rainwater off our barn and house into the kitchen and bathroom.

Then, 'long about 1923, somebody back East invented this thing called a hot-water heater. Daddy figured Mama ought to have one, only we couldn't afford it. That didn't stop him. He wrapped copper pipe around a potbellied stove. Mama had to stoke the fire, turn on the tractor motor that ran the pump, then come back in the house and turn on the bathtub spigot. She said it would be easier just to heat water on the stove like most farm folk did.

Daddy didn't like all the time it took to milk the dairy cows, either. He rigged up an automatic milker. Said it was gonna revolutionize the whole dairy industry. Only, when he hooked it up, Bessy went to pitching and bellowing and tore her stall apart. Broke three of Daddy's ribs in the process.

Fact was, most of Daddy's inventions didn't work. The one thing that turned out pretty good was his hay baler. He got one from a fella up in Iowa. But instead of using thin rope or string to bind the bales, he got him some fine gauged wire. Lots of the bales fell apart, but some looked right fine. Three years in a row, Daddy won a blue ribbon at the state fair for his hay.

Figure that's what brought the tall, slender guy name of James Dole to our farm. Because it wasn't long after the state fair that he showed up to offer Daddy a job on his pineapple plantation.

After they walked around the farm and Daddy showed him some of his things, they come back to the house. Daddy was up front with the guy. He told him as how he knew absolutely nothing about pineapples and how most of his inventions didn't work, anyway.

James Dole wanted him to come even more. "Not only do I need a man of foresight, but one of integrity," he'd said. I didn't know what that meant, but I kept listening anyway. "Of all the men I've interviewed, you have been the most honest about telling me of your failures as well as your successes. I prize your honesty and integrity, even more than your inventions, Mr. Priddle."

Daddy had been excited. All his tinkering and inventing was on his own time and with his own money. Now, someone was actually gonna pay him to do what he loved doing.

Mama was excited. She talked of an island paradise. She could see a hammock tied between two palm trees that gently swayed in the warm breeze.

I was excited. I'd never been to an island. Shoot, I'd never even seen the ocean. But here I was, going to a place where no one at Pioneer School had ever been. Bet no one in even the big town of Chickasha— no, probably in the whole state of Oklahoma—bet none of them had ever been to a little island out in the middle of the Pacific Ocean.

Grandma just shook her head and mumbled, "Out of the frying pan, into the fire."

The evening before we'd left, I'd heard her talking to Mama while they fixed supper.

"Don't know what I done wrong, raising the boy," she'd said. "He's smart and quick. Ain't no arguing that. But he just don't have a level head on his shoulders. Always wanting to change stuff. Always wanting to make things better. Never satisfied with his lot in life."

She'd looked around one way, and before she looked the other, I managed to jerk behind the doorjamb where she couldn't see me.

"Now, Helen." Her voice was a whisper. "I never thought I'd say something like this. But if things get too bad—you leave that knot-head son of mine. Just pack up you and the boy and get yourselves back home, here. You understand? Just leave him."

There had been a long, long silence. I'd leaned around the doorjamb to see what was going on. Mama was hugging Grandma.

"He's got his faults, Mabel," she'd told her with tears in her eyes. "But I love him! If he wants to go to the island, and it makes him happy, I'm going. If he wants to go past the island and clean off the face of the earth, I'd follow him and not think a thing of it. We'll be fine. You quit your fretting."

"What about John?" Grandma had asked.

Mama sighed. "In a couple of years, John will be old enough to make his own decisions. He might stay with Keith and me, might come back here. Who knows what he's gonna do? There's one thing I do want for him. A thing I hope for him more than anything else."

"And what's that?"

"Love." Mama had smiled. "Someday, I hope John finds the kind of love that Keith and I have for one another. Nothing else he does or is really matters— just so long as he's got that."

The schooner rose again, hesitated a second, then started its fall. I tightened my grip. I never felt so sick. The muscles in my stomach jerked down as tight as my grip on the rail.

"Love," I mocked the word inside my head. The only thing I love is ground—good, firm, solid earth. If I can just live long enough to get my feet on . . .

I threw up again.

Chapter 2

"Love."

I sneered.

"No way, not this ole boy."

At fourteen going on fifteen, there weren't a whole lot I knew. But there were a couple of things I *did* know.

First off, love had something to do with girls. And if a fella had any sense at all, he didn't have *nothing* to do with no girl! Now, looking was just fine. I mean they *were* interesting critters. Only, don't mess with 'em!

Once, back in second grade, I'd played with Susie Potter. She was a cute little thing with an upturned nose and long, blond pigtails.

We had come in from the playground one day and David Whittaker, who was in fourth grade, had seen us holding hands. He and the other guys had started singing:

> John and Susie,
> Sittin' in a tree,

K-I-S-S-I-N-G!
First comes love,
Then comes marriage,
Then comes Johnny
With a baby carriage.

It had embarrassed the dickens outa me! Every time I'd so much as look at Susie Potter, it started all over again.

When I told Mama and Daddy about it, they said not to pay any attention to the guys at school. They told me just to ignore them and they'd quit. Then after supper one night, I overheard them talking in the living room. Mama said how "cute and sweet" it was that I had a girlfriend.

It didn't take a genius to figure out that girls were nothing but trouble.

Then there was cousin Molly. She come down every summer from Oklahoma City with Daddy's sister Elizabeth and her husband. Getting Molly on a horse was like trying to lift two grain sacks and a bale of hay. She was nothing but dead weight. Once I got her behind me on the saddle, she liked to wrap herself around my middle. She'd squeeze and giggle, then she'd go to squealing and hollering like a pig stuck in the mud—almost break my eardrums.

And last year at the church social, Amanda Burke latched onto me. She kept wanting to hold my hand. It was like getting rid of snot. I kept wiggling and jerking and flipping my hand, but I still couldn't get her off me. Every time I'd get loose from her, she'd just grab again. I finally got my hand free, and darned if she didn't latch onto my arm. Liked to never got away from her.

Charlie Eagle was even worse off. Charlie had been my best friend ever since first grade. We done all sorts of things together—talking, hunting and fishing, riding horses—everything. Then a few months ago, at the school Christmas party, Beth Simms got to making goo-goo eyes at him. Charlie done went and started looking back!

Poor Charlie hadn't been the same since. She batted her eyes—he swooned. She smiled—he wiggled. She snapped her fingers—he might near broke his neck trying to jump. He ate lunch with her instead of eating with me. He spent his time talking to her instead of spending time with me. Beth Simms was all Charlie could think about or talk about. Poor Charlie.

Girls were nothing but trouble. Staying away from them was one thing I knew for sure.

Another thing I knew for sure . . .

If I ever got my feet on dry land again, I would never—and I do mean NEVER—get anywhere near the ocean!

It hadn't been bad at first. The train trip had been wonderful. I'd never seen mountains before. I'd seen the Wichita Mountains, but they weren't even good hills compared to the Rockies. I'd never seen streams that were blue and clear instead of the muddy, reddish brown of Oklahoma dirt. I used to think Oklahoma City was big. That had been until our train pulled into San Francisco.

James Dole had booked passage for us on a cargo ship called *The Essex*. During the first two weeks it wasn't so bad. Then, five days ago, we'd hit the storm. The steamer was big. The storm was bigger.

For three days my head rolled, my stomach rolled, and my eyes rolled. I'd never been so sick in my life. For three days, I threw up everything I took in—and then some. Fact was, I felt like I'd thrown up everything but my toenails.

Three days! Three days of throwing up and being sick as a dog and asking God to let me die. It was nearly noon on that third day when I'd heard one of the sailors yell:

"Hawaii!"

People scurried about. They were all excited and talking about how green it was and how tall the mountains were.

I'd tried to look, only I'd thrown up again.

After I'd puked about three more times, I remember hearing Mama's voice.

"What's that big, pink building over yonder?"

"That's the Moano Hotel," one of the crewmen answered. "And see all that rock and dirt just up the beach from it?"

I didn't even try to look.

"That's where they're gonna build an even bigger hotel. It's called the Royal Hawaiian and ain't even due to open until 1927. Thing's gonna be huge."

"I heard that a California company is building a liner," a woman said, "only to carry passengers from the mainland to the Hawaiian Islands. You know, for vacations and the like."

The crewman made a little snorting noise. "I just can't picture it," he'd said politely. "I mean, the volcanoes on the big island are interesting, but not that many people come to look at 'em. And as far as places to stay, who's gonna want to stay in a hotel built in the middle of Waikiki swamp?"

I didn't care if it was a swamp. If I could ever get off this stupid boat, I was gonna fall on my knees and kiss the very ground—swamp or not.

We docked at Honolulu. I didn't fall on my knees and kiss the ground. There wasn't any ground. Just a wood dock that smelled of creosote, and so many people bustling around, if I'd got down to kiss the ground, somebody probably would have stepped on my head or my hands. We stayed in Honolulu just long enough for Daddy to go to the Dole Pineapple factory. Next thing I knew, we were on Mr. Dole's private yacht.

I didn't even have time to get over being sick, and we were right back out on the ocean.

There was one last thing I knew—that there was a God. It was one of the few things Daddy and Mama and Grandma *all* agreed on.

I glanced up from the rail and looked into the blue sky.

"Please, God," I whispered. "Either let me get on land or let me die. It don't matter which. But just do one or the other—quick!"

Chapter 3

Well, there were three things I knew. First, I *knew* to stay away from girls. And I *knew* that if I ever got to dry land, I'd never get near the ocean again. But, to be right honest, I was beginning to have my doubts about the third thing I knew—about God.

That's 'cause it took us so long to get the boat stopped.

Compared to the harbor in Honolulu, the one where we landed next was absolutely tiny. There were no buildings at all, just a big wooden dock that connected to another narrow dock. The whole thing wasn't much bigger than the cow lot back on our farm.

Christopher Sanches was the captain of Mr. Dole's schooner. He was from Portugal.

Captain Sanches shouted at his first mate, a short man with brown skin and almond-shaped eyes called Ching Lung. They slid the schooner right up alongside the wooden dock, as smooth as a hot knife slicing through fresh butter.

Once the schooner was secure, Captain Sanches

and Ching Lung lowered a wooden plank. I was the first one off. Like the dock at Honolulu, the stink of creosote clung to the wood. I walked to the end of the dock and jumped to the ground. I didn't stand there long because the waves lapped up and got my shoes wet. A steep, rocky hill stretched out in front of me. I had to walk quite a ways to find anything but bare rock. There was no grass or nothing. Finally, I found a clump of trees and sat down in the shade.

I didn't bother to look back. I was so sick, I didn't even want to look in the direction of the water. I figured if I sat really still and stared at the ground and the trees, maybe my eyes would quit rolling.

The tree near where I sat looked a lot like the mesquite trees down by Wichita Falls in Texas. There was cactus everywhere, too. The ground was red—just like the soil back home—only full of little rocks.

Man alive, I thought, *if this is an island paradise, I'd sure hate to see that place the preachers are always threatening us with in church.* Hawaii was supposed to be palm trees swaying in the breeze and white sandy beaches and pretty girls running around in grass skirts or something.

Lanai looked more like Oklahoma. It was hot and dry. There were mesquite trees and red dirt and . . .

Suddenly a movement caught my eye. I froze. Not even letting my eyes blink, I held my breath and watched.

A big tom turkey strutted from behind a pile of brush. He was a wild turkey, dark feathered and sporting a fine beard. Behind him, two hens appeared. They paused to peck at the ground, then scurried along to hide in another pile of brush.

All at once the tom's head shot straight up in the air. He spun and raced across a little opening. The hens followed, running a ways before they spread their big dark wings and took to flight.

I hadn't moved a bit, so I glanced around to see what had spooked them.

A horse stood not ten feet behind me. She was a sorrel with one white stocking. She was short and looked more like a Welsh pony than a horse. The horse pawed the ground and gave a loud snort when I leaned around the tree.

When the girl on the mare's back saw me, she gave a little jerk. Then she smiled, and deep dimples broke the smooth line of her golden brown cheek.

"Hi."

"Hi," I said back.

She nodded toward the schooner.

"Your *makua* the new *alii?*"

Frowning, I tilted my head to the side.

"Huh?"

"Your father," she said. "Is he the new alii?"

With a grunt, I struggled to my feet and took a step toward her. I was still wobbly and weak from being so seasick.

"What did you say?"

She put a hand to her mouth. I could see a flush across her bronze face.

"I'm sorry," she laughed. "I've spent too much time

with my grandfather. He does not speak English too good. *Makua* means 'father,' and *alii* is the word for 'chief' or 'boss.' I asked if your father was the new boss."

I shook my head and took another step closer.

"No. He's just gonna be working for Mr. Dole on his plantation. Not a boss or a foreman or nothing."

The smile left her face. Even without the warm grin, she was still kind of pretty. Her long black hair was straight and came down below her shoulders. She had on a crisp white blouse and a blue cotton skirt. The horse stomped her foot when I walked closer.

"My name's John Priddle. I'm from Oklahoma." She didn't say anything. For some strange reason, I felt kind of awkward. "You from around here?"

The instant I asked, I felt my eyes roll inside my head. Boy, what a dumb thing to say.

The girl nodded.

"Yes. I live with my grandfather, *makai*," she said, pointing.

"What's his name, Mack? Mack Eye? Is Eye your last name?"

She sighed and shook her head. "No, *makai* means 'toward the sea'." She nodded at a small ridge. "We live by ocean, beyond that little hill. My grandfather's name is Makalii Pukui."

She smiled at me. I couldn't help smiling back. I wanted to talk to her, but for the life of me, I couldn't think of anything to say. For some strange reason, I felt kind of nervous and twittery inside. I looked down at the red dirt and sort of shifted from one foot to the other before I looked up at her again.

"That's a mighty fine looking animal you're riding."

You talk about "Out of the frying pan, into the fire"!

Chapter 4

"All I said was, that's a mighty fine looking animal you're riding," I tried to explain when Daddy asked me why I had a horse.

"That's all?"

"Yes, sir. That's all! First thing I know, she hopped down and handed me the reins. I was petting the mare and trying to figure out something else to say to the girl, and when I looked up . . . she was gone!"

"Gone?" Daddy cocked an eyebrow.

"Gone," I repeated. The mare pawed the ground and tossed her head. "I mean, like one minute she was there and the next minute, it was just me and this horse. I don't know what happened."

"I don't know what happened, neither," Daddy said, frowning. "But you got to find her and give it back."

Captain Sanches stepped up beside us. I guess he'd heard part of what was going on.

"Pretty girl? About your age, maybe a little younger?"

"Yes, sir."

"Long black hair and all dressed for school?"

"Black hair about down to here," I reached around and marked across my back with my hand.

With a smile, Captain Sanches nodded.

"Sounds like Carol Pukui. She and her grandfather live over on Hulopoe Bay. Old man's a fisherman."

I offered the reins to him.

"You know where she lives. Could you . . ."

Rough, callused hands closed over mine, wrapping my grip about the reins.

"To return the gift—to give the horse back—it would be not a good thing."

I frowned and tilted my head to the side. Captain Sanches's smile was gentle and patient.

"Makalii Pukui is an old, old man. He has raised his granddaughter in the old ways—the old Hawaiian traditions. You admired something that belonged to her, so she gave it to you.

"The Hawaiians are a very generous and giving people," Captain Sanches explained. "Especially the ones who live on the outer islands and haven't been, how do you say . . . ah . . . 'jaded' by big-city life, like some in Honolulu."

"Huh?" Daddy and I both asked at the same time.

The captain let go of my hands and put an arm on my shoulder. "Granted, a horse is a little much. Usually a gift would be a flower lei or some handmade item. Nonetheless, generosity is a matter of pride to these people."

"But . . . but . . ." I stammered.

"We can't keep her horse," Daddy said. "It wouldn't be right."

Captain Sanches shrugged. "The decision is yours. But to return the horse would be an insult. It would hurt the old man's feelings as well as bring shame to his granddaughter. Now, George Munro has a couple of horses, not far from his house. You could keep it there and . . ."

"Captain Sanches," Daddy interrupted. "It just doesn't seem right to . . ."

"Keith," Mama broke in. I guess she'd been standing behind us for a while. We didn't notice her until she stepped between Daddy and me to put an arm on our shoulders.

"We're new to this place. Their customs are different from ours, and it's going to take us some time to catch on to things. I think Captain Sanches knows the people and the islands much better than we do. We should follow his advice. I mean, I'd hate to start out the first day in our new home by offending someone."

"But . . . but . . ."

Mama ignored my stammering. She took Captain Sanches's hand and shook it. "Thank you for explaining the custom to us. Are there other things we should know? Other customs or traditions we might not be familiar with?"

They talked. I just stood there with my mouth open. What was I gonna do with a horse? I liked horses. I loved riding. But what was I gonna do with this horse? Why didn't I keep my big mouth shut?

A man named Paul Jacobs came about twenty minutes later in a fancy new car. Three men in a beat-up-looking farm truck followed him. Mr. Jacobs introduced himself to Mama and Daddy as the foreman of the Lanai Pineapple Plantation. He smiled and shook our hands like he was pumping water from a well. I never seen anybody act so happy to meet someone he didn't even know. The men in the truck loaded our stuff, and Captain Sanches went with them instead of staying around to visit.

Mr. Jacobs seemed right tickled when Mama and Daddy told him about the horse. Fact was, he seemed downright thrilled. He told one of the men to drive the truck and instructed another to take my horse and put it in George Munro's horse lot.

"You can keep the horse at Munro's place, but far as I'm concerned, the old man's loony as a bedbug," he cautioned Daddy. "Be wise to keep your wife and boy as far away from him as possible."

We climbed in his shiny automobile.

"What kind of car is this?" Daddy asked.

"She's a 1924 Chrysler," Mr. Jacobs boasted. "Maxwell Motor Corporation just came out with them last year. Jim Dole has two and there are only four others in the whole entire Hawaii Territory."

As we puttered and chugged up the steep hill that led from the bay, we waved good-bye to Captain

Sanches. From the front of his schooner, he waved and called, "Aloha!"

I liked Captain Sanches.

Mr. Jacobs wanted to know everything there was to know about Daddy and his inventions. He asked Mama what the weather was like in Oklahoma and what the land looked like. He even asked me about my school and if I liked to play baseball. His boy, Ted, was in eighth grade, and he was sure that we would be best friends.

When we were about halfway up the hill, I noticed someone walking ahead of us on the road. We sped closer, and I could see the girl with the long black hair. I wanted to ask if we could give her a ride, but before I could even get a word in, we whooshed past her. A cloud of red dust swirled. I guess it was so thick she didn't even see me wave.

I twisted around in the seat and got up on my knees. We went around one curve then another as we wound our way up the hill. I felt sorry for the girl. Not only did she have to walk to school instead of riding her horse, but now, her white blouse was all covered with red dust. We were quite a ways off when the old farm truck with our luggage finally came into view.

When I saw the men stop and watched the girl climb onto the back of the truck, I smiled.

But when I turned around and sat back down in the seat, I could see Mr. Jacobs's face in the mirror. He was watching, too. Only, he wasn't smiling.

Chapter 5

By the time Mr. Jacobs dropped us at our new home, I was feeling a little sick again. It would sure be nice to get my feet on firm ground and not be moving all the time.

"Never felt so welcomed in a place in my life," Mama said as we watched Mr. Jacobs drive off.

"Me neither." Daddy shook his head. "He was so tickled to meet us, I was afraid there for a second, that he was gonna drop down and kiss our feet or something."

Mama sat cross-legged on the floor, sorting through some of the boxes.

"He wanted to know all there was to know about us and John. And he wasn't the least bit bashful when it come to telling about the island and the plantation. Never met a more friendly, open fella."

Daddy nodded.

"Reckon we made a good move, coming here." He shoved a box in my direction. "Your jeans." Then he went right back talking to Mama. "I spent some time up on deck, visiting with Captain Sanches after you and John went to bed last night. He said that there's people from all over the world living on Oahu. You know, where the steamer put in?"

Mama nodded without looking up from the box she was digging in.

"He says that for the most part, they get along right well. People work and play just fine. The Hawaii Territory is a good place, and there's lots of good people living here."

Mama looked up.

"Mr. Jacobs didn't mention much about the other people on our island. What did Captain Sanches say about Lanai?"

"Well, let's see. He told me it was eighteen miles long and thirteen miles wide. The highest place is called Lanaihale. It's 3,370 feet above sea level. And by next year, when the south field is finished, it's gonna be the biggest pineapple plantation in the whole, entire world."

He took another step toward his room.

"Keith?" Mama called after him. "What did he say about the people?"

"Come to think of it," he answered. "He didn't."

The words didn't hang in the air for long. There was too much to do and see. We spent the rest of that week unloading, putting stuff away, and exploring our new surroundings.

Lanai City was what most folks in Oklahoma would call a little farm town. There weren't any of the tall office buildings or street cars or crowds of people that it takes to make a city. Fact was, we hardly saw any people at all.

We walked past a bunch of houses. They were what Daddy called "cracker boxes"—just wood frame houses, all sort of square and boxlike. "Nothing fancy," he'd said. "But can you imagine? James Dole told me he provides rent-free housing for all his workers. A fella sure can't complain about a deal like that." We went past the school and past the Mercantile, then back home.

Although there were some fairly tall trees on the ridge north of Lanai City, where the mountain rose up, there were no palm trees swaying in the breeze for Mama to hang a hammock. The ground looked like a plowed field, only cluttered with small rocks and pebbles. There was no grass. The only trees down here were some sort of little pines that were about as high as my knee.

Our first week, other than moving into a beautiful new home, well . . .

Lanai wasn't all that exciting.

The next week wasn't much better.

Daddy spent Monday and Tuesday riding around with Mr. Jacobs. Mr. Jacobs was real concerned that our new home and everything in it was to our liking. He was just as friendly as could be. Only, Daddy did nothing but watch him pour different colored dyes into little streams near the top of the mountain. Then stand around while the water and the dye disappeared into the rock. "They spent over a million dollars to run a pipeline from the far side of the island," Daddy had told us. "And they have already started on a big reservoir. Don't know why Mr. Jacobs is trying to track where the water goes. Judging by the big dam they're building, and all the water they already have, there should be plenty for everyone in Lanai City, plus enough to flood the whole island if someone took a mind to."

Wednesday and Thursday, Daddy drove around with Mr. Jacobs, while he tried to get some of the Hawaiians to sell their land to Mr. Dole and the Hapco Pineapple Company. When Hawaii became a territory, the government had given allotments to the native Hawaiians. Most of them had already sold their land, but a few still lived on Lanai. Mr. Jacobs wanted *all* of the island for Mr. Dole. Daddy said that when Mr. Jacobs made his offers to buy the land, he wasn't nearly as nice and friendly with the Hawaiians as he was with us. It bothered Daddy—just a little.

"I can't learn about pineapples or how to improve the operation from the front seat of Paul Jacobs's Chrysler," he told Mama at supper, Thursday night. "I have to be out in the fields with the other men. I have to have my hands on things—work with things—before I can see what needs to be improved. Tomorrow morning, I'm gonna tell Mr. Jacobs that!"

Mama nodded her agreement. "I've been down to the Mercantile every day to buy groceries," Mama began. "Carmine Jacobs is sweet and friendly. She wants me to come and work with her at the store."

Daddy's forkful of mashed potatoes froze right at his lips. "They're that busy?" he asked.

Mama smiled. "Not really. I think she's lonely. But it pays twenty-five cents a day. And I really need something to do."

Daddy stuffed the potatoes in his mouth and frowned at her. Mama shrugged.

"Back home, there were always chores and things. In the spring, there was the garden to tend. Here . . . well, there's nothing for me to do. Besides, like I said, Carmine seems sweet."

I watched the lump in Daddy's throat when the mashed potatoes went down. He smiled and gave a little shrug. "Sounds okay to me," he said finally.

Everybody ate a little longer. Suddenly I noticed their eyes on me.

"How was your week, John?" Daddy smiled. "Enjoy your first week of school?"

I blinked and tried to smile back.

And, in that instant, it was like the whole, entire, HORRIBLE week flashed through my mind's eye.

Chapter 6

The one thing I had most wanted was to find a new friend. Someone like Charlie Eagle. That's why I had been so excited about starting school.

Monday morning, it rained.

"Winter and spring are the rainy seasons on the islands," the man with a strange accent informed Mama when she introduced us that morning. "The rains should have subsided by this time, however . . ." He made a little coughing sound and sneered down at our feet. "The Orientals have a custom of leaving their shoes outside when they enter a home or building. During the rainy season, we have adopted that custom. This keeps our building clean and neat."

Now most times—leastways back home when someone introduces themselves—folks shake your hand and tell who they are. This guy just commenced talking about rain and shoes. Mama introduced herself again. The man said his name was Mr. Foster. He was from Europe and would be my teacher.

While he and Mama visited, I scurried back to the door and put my shoes alongside the others. I didn't mind being barefoot. Fact, going to school and not having to wear shoes sounded kind of neat. Then I noticed the hole where my big toe stuck through my sock. These were my best pair, and now I was going to have to sit around school all day with my toe hanging out.

". . . and he'll need a white shirt and dark trousers," I heard Mr. Foster say when I walked up. Mama nodded toward me.

"Would Levi's work? John doesn't really have any dark slacks."

Mr. Foster's nose curled.

"Well, if that is all he has, I suppose . . ."

Mr. Foster was tall and lanky. He wore a tie and coat. His white shirt was starched. As I listened to him talk, I figured his underwear must have been starched, too.

Mama told me she'd have lunch ready at noon, then left. Mr. Foster pointed (with a stiff finger) at the classroom door, and I walked in.

The room was big, but there were only about fifteen desks in the whole thing. Instead of being divided up by grade, like in Oklahoma, the kids were in clumps, with first-graders through eighth-graders all sitting together. There was a pasty-white kid with red hair right in front of Mr. Foster's desk. A little ways behind him were the rest of the kids. All had black hair and dark faces. Their brown skin reminded me of Charlie Eagle and his family. Though I knew I wasn't as pasty white as the red-haired kid, I sure felt like I stood out from the crowd.

"Ladies and gentlemen," Mr. Foster announced stiffly. "May I have your attention so that I may introduce our new student?"

Everyone stopped what they were doing and glanced toward me. Without looking down, I eased my left foot over the top of my right so I could hide my big toe.

"This is John Priddle. He comes to us from Oklahoma. Does anyone know where Oklahoma is?"

I thought I was gonna die. Not only did I have to stand here, with the whole class looking at my big toe, but I had to wait while someone walked to the big map on the wall and pointed at Oklahoma.

The girl who had given me the horse was sitting by herself in the back of the room. She raised her hand. Mr. Foster kept looking around. Nobody else moved. Still he waited. Finally, he gave a stiff sigh.

"All right, Carol."

She got up from her desk and walked across the room. Everyone was still watching me, though. I tried to smile and look pleasant. The girl picked up a yardstick and pointed. Inside my head, I was thinking, *Boy I wish I was back there—back in Oklahoma—right now!*

"Good guess, Carol," Mr. Foster didn't smile. "Does anyone know the capital of Oklahoma?"

Except for the little kids, almost every hand in the room went up.

"Ted Jacobs," Mr. Foster called.

Ted Jacobs was the pasty, white kid with the red hair. He stood up from his desk, looking almost as stiff as Mr. Foster.

"Oklahoma City?"

"That's right." The corners of Mr. Foster's mouth went up just a fraction. (Any farther and his face might have cracked.) "Excellent, Ted! I'm most impressed."

It was all I could do to keep from rolling my eyes and shaking my head. I mean, Oklahoma City wasn't the hardest to put together with a state. Even the dumbest kid could get that one right off.

To make matters worse, Mr. Foster said, "Does anyone have any questions for Mr. Priddle concerning life in Oklahoma?"

Nobody raised a hand. He waited. Finally, the girl with the long black hair raised her arm. But Mr. Foster waited and waited and waited. When no one else raised a hand, he cleared his throat. "Very well, if no one has questions, I shall ask."

So . . . I had to stand there while he asked one question after another. I teetered on one foot, 'cause my other was covering up the hole in my sock. At long last, he left the room to get me a desk. I stood there, with my foot over the hole in my sock—grinning and looking like a total idiot.

I had on Levi's instead of dark slacks, my big toe stuck out the hole in my sock, and—if all that wasn't bad enough—Mr. Foster put my desk right in front of the class, next to Ted Jacobs's. I sure hoped Ted was easier to talk to than his dad.

We read and did math and read some more. When it was time for lunch, I got my shoes and ran home to eat. It had stopped raining, so I gobbled my food down so fast, I almost choked. I wanted to get back and see what was going on at school. Maybe Ted Jacobs was okay. Maybe he would be my best friend.

Ted Jacobs was the exact opposite of his dad. Mr. Jacobs talked and seemed friendly as could be. Ted *never talked*. He never smiled. All he did was throw his baseball on the roof of the school and catch it when it rolled down. He acted as interested and friendly as a rattlesnake.

After a time I gave up on Ted Jacobs and started trying to make friends with some of the other kids. Maybe, without Mr. Foster around, they'd ask me questions about Oklahoma. Now that I had my shoes on, I didn't mind. The boys were right in the middle of a baseball game. I watched a while, but when I moved in their direction, they stopped playing and wandered toward the school. I didn't even get a chance to ask if I could play.

Making new friends might be a little tougher than I thought. Maybe tomorrow would be different.

Tomorrow wasn't any different. Neither was the next day, or the day after that, or . . .

My eyes fluttered. Mama and Daddy were still staring at me from across the dinner table.

"John," Daddy repeated. "How was your first week of school?"

I didn't lie to my folks. But how was I gonna tell Mama and Daddy how miserable school was? How was I gonna tell them how lonely it was not to have anyone to play with or talk to? There was a gulping sound inside my head when I swallowed.

"It was just fine," I lied.

That night, I tried to convince myself I really hadn't lied to them. Daddy was gonna get Mr. Jacobs to let him start working in the pineapple fields with the other guys. Mama was gonna start to work with Mrs. Jacobs at the Mercantile—so she'd have something to do.

Me . . . well, I could make some changes, too. I could spend some time with the guys. Make them be friends with me. So it really wouldn't be a lie—not if I made things better. Then the first week of school really would be "just fine."

Chapter 7

Friday, right before lunch, I waited until most of the kids left the room. I mustered my courage and marched right up to Mr. Foster and asked if I could sit with the other boys and girls instead of at the front.

Somehow he managed to laugh without changing the stiff expression on his face.

"It has been my experience," he whispered, "that intellectually, whites are far superior to the darker races. Thus, I find it advisable to separate you and Mr. Jacobs so that I may give you the special attention of which you are so deserving."

When I got home for lunch, I repeated what Mr. Foster had said, almost word for word, and asked Mama what the heck he meant.

Mama's mouth kind of gaped open. Then her eyes got tight and squinty. Finally, she sighed and shook her head.

"Whatever he means," Mama said gruffly. "he *is* your new teacher, and . . ."

"But I don't want to sit by Ted," I interrupted. "He

don't talk. He's got about as much personality as a wet mop, and besides he keeps peeking at my math paper. I can hear, when the other kids are working, and they know a lot of stuff. I bet half the class is smarter than Ted Jacobs.

"You remember the little girl, the one who gave me the horse? She's got her hand up all the time. She's real smart. Only, he won't call on her. Reckon it's 'cause her English ain't always too hot, but . . ."

"Isn't too hot," Mama corrected.

"Huh?"

"Isn't," Mama repeated. "And you're a fine one to be complaining about someone's English. When did all this 'ain't' stuff start?"

"*Isn't* too hot," I repeated. "Anyhow, she sometimes leaves out words and stuff. Remember how Captain Sanches said she lived with her grandfather? I think she does right good for someone who ain't . . ." I caught myself before Mama could say anything. "For someone who hasn't been around a lot of people who speak English. And like I said, she's real smart but Mr. Foster ignores her. He's wrong, Mama. Besides, I want to be with the rest of the kids and make new friends and . . ."

"Right or wrong, Mr. Foster *is* your teacher," Mama broke in. "You'll do what your teacher says—just like back home. Now eat your dinner."

"But . . ."

"Eat!"

*   *   *

Right or wrong, I was still determined. If Mr. Foster wouldn't let me make friends by sitting with the guys in school, then I'd *make* them play with me at recess.

When I got back to school, the guys were playing baseball out on the field. Just like what happened the last four days, when I started toward them, they broke up and headed for the building.

Only this time, instead of giving up and going off alone, I followed them. It was almost like a chase game. The faster I walked, the faster they walked. When I followed them clean up to the front door, they kind of fanned out in all directions like a covey of quail.

A kid about my age and size, named Robert, got separated from the others. Like a wolf circling its prey, I finally cornered him near the side of the building.

"Robert. Hey, Robert! Hold up a second."

He stopped, with his back pressed into the side of the school. There he stood, like a trapped rat, while I closed in on him.

"There's a couple of things I been wanting to ask you."

He didn't look up. He just stood there, staring at the ground and nodding his head.

"On my way home from school, I been kinda looking around for somebody to play with. But all I see is little kids and girls. Where do you guys go after school and on Saturdays to play?"

Ever so slowly, he peeked up at me.

"After school, to play?" he asked very quietly.

"Yeah. Where do all the guys go? What do you do?"
Again, he looked down at the ground.

"We go to pineapple fields. We work hard."

I felt myself draw back.

"All the guys? Even the little ones?"

"When eight or nine," he answered without looking up. "We all work in fields. Work hard."

He tried to move away. I stepped in front of him.

"What about Sundays? You don't work on Sundays do you?"

He shook his head. "Sunday, go to gardens."

"Gardens?"

He nodded. "Family have garden on far side of island. Raise sweet potatoes, rice, and beans. We all help in gardens after church."

Mr. Foster stepped on the porch and rang the bell, calling us in from lunch. Robert took off like a shot. I chased after him and grabbed his arm before he got to the steps.

"Look," I said, turning him to face me. "There's one other thing. Every time I try to play with you guys or talk to you, all of you take off like I got the plague or something. How come you don't want me to play ball with you and stuff?"

For the first time, Robert looked me in the eye. He frowned and tilted his head to the side. Quickly he looked away.

"You are *haole*."

He pulled his arm free and scurried inside.

*   *   *

Mama and Daddy weren't home from work, so I settled in on my math assignment for Monday. There were only about twenty long-division problems, but I was just finishing up when I heard Mama open the front door.

Ordinarily, it wouldn't take me that long to do twenty division problems. But I kept trying to think things out while working on my math. First off, Mr. Foster wouldn't let me sit with the rest of the class. Second, they wouldn't play with me at recess, 'cause I was "holy," or "haole," some word like that.

Mama started supper, and when I asked her, she said, "I know what *holy* is. But," she added with a sly smile, "I doubt that's what he was calling you. I have no idea what *haole* means, you'll have to ask your dad."

"Reckon I could work with him and the other guys in the pineapple fields?"

"You'll have to ask your father that, too," she answered, tilting her head toward the door. "Think that's him now."

I stretched my neck, listening. I heard the sound of a motor and sprinted to the porch. Daddy didn't even look up when I opened the door and said hi. He sort of waddled into the house, across the kitchen, and straight to Mama.

"What's wrong, Keith?" She frowned. "What's the matter?"

Daddy pointed down. Both of us looked at the brown blotches and spots on the legs of his bib overalls.

"Had my first lesson on pineapples today." He smiled. Only it looked more like the smile a sick calf would give than a smile from my daddy.

"Are those pineapple stains?" Mama asked.

Daddy shook his head. He unhooked the straps on his overalls. "José de los Santos, he's the guy in charge of the crew I worked with today. He sent me back into the house this morning to put on another pair of pants." Underneath his overalls, he had on a second pair. He flipped the straps on them back over his shoulder. "Two pair of pants didn't help."

With that, he kind of wiggled. Both overalls landed in a clump about his feet. In his boxer shorts, he stood there and we all looked down.

"Oh, Keith," Mama gasped.

"Oh, Daddy," I whimpered.

"Not pineapple stains," Daddy sighed. "Blood."

From the hem of his boxer shorts clean down to his ankles, Daddy's legs were scratched and poked and bloody. It looked like he'd been on the losing end of a fight with a bobcat or something.

Mama had him sit down. While she untied one shoe, I fought with the other.

Once we had his shoes off, we were real careful pulling his overalls past his feet. Daddy kind of sighed and slumped back in the chair when we finally got his clothes off.

Mama spun around and turned the heat off under the stove. Then she knelt beside Daddy and patted his arm.

"We don't have any medicine," she soothed. "You

get into the bath. I'll run over to the Jacobs's house and see if they have any zinc ointment."

I started to volunteer to go get it for her. But I guess she thought I was still asking about working in the pineapple fields, 'cause all I managed to get out of my mouth was "Mama . . ."

In the blink of an eye, she spun on me. She pointed a finger like she was aiming down the barrel of a gun. "Forget it," she snapped. "Don't even ask!"

Chapter 8

Mama tried to get Daddy to stay home Sunday morning. But Daddy assured us he was fine. Besides, we had promised the Jacobses we'd come for Sunday dinner.

Back home we went to the First Christian Church. But there were only two churches on Lanai—Methodist and Catholic. As far as the preaching and the songs and stuff went, the Methodists were right close.

The preacher's name was Mr. Scott. He had white hair and dark eyes that seemed to fit in just right with his fire-and-brimstone sermon—the same kind of preaching Reverend Thornton did back home.

The big difference was that hardly anybody was there. The Jacobses sat on one end of the front pew and Mr. Foster on the other. Behind them, a man named du Chance sat with his wife. He was a chemist from France. Another chemist sat on the same pew with them, but Daddy didn't know his name. There was an empty row, then five Filipino guys in the next. Three more empty rows and then about twenty or so Hawaiians sat at the very back of the church. I could tell they were Hawaiian 'cause of the bright, flowery dresses the women wore and 'cause Carol Pukui sat with them. I knew she was Hawaiian.

We sat on the third row, by ourselves.

After church, we walked over to the Jacobses'. Daddy was hurting some. He walked kind of stiff-legged. Still, he did his best to smile and pretend he was interested in what Paul Jacobs had to say. And as usual, Paul Jacobs had a *bunch* to say.

"Most of the Flips go over to the Catholic church with Father Jenkins," he started as soon as we left. "The Catholics are by far the largest congregation and have the biggest church. That's probably because most of our *kanakas* are Flips. There are a few Hawaiians who go over there, too. For the most part, they're just heathens. Too lazy or backward to get off their duffs and go to church. Japs are about the same way. They built them a shrine up the mountain there." He pointed. "Idol worshipers if you ask me. Bunch of heathens, like the local natives. Now, if it were up to me . . ."

"I figure the way a man chooses to worship is pretty much up to *him*." Daddy's voice was sharp and loud. It kind of surprised me. I guess it surprised Paul Jacobs, too. He stopped dead in his tracks and turned to Daddy.

"What did you say?"

Daddy's voice was softer, but he stared Mr. Jacobs straight in the eye and didn't blink once.

"I said the way a man chooses to worship is pretty much up to him," he repeated. "Ben Eagle was my best friend back in Oklahoma. He was a deacon at the First Baptist Church in a little settlement called Laverty." Daddy turned and started calmly but stiffly up the street. "Ben's a right good Christian man. Thing is, he's also full-blood Kiowa. His dad and granddad brought him up believing in 'the Great Spirit' and the old ceremonial ways. But according to Ben, the Great Spirit and God are right close with one another. Fact is, he told me one time that he figured it was two different names for the same thing."

Paul Jacobs stopped again and folded his arms.

"And your point?"

Mr. Jacobs stood there, frowning. When Daddy didn't stop, he followed along. Daddy shrugged and glanced back over his shoulder.

"My point is that I didn't know whether he was right or wrong. I ain't smart enough or wise enough to judge another man for his beliefs. I know the way I believe and it helps me. I figure every man of faith feels the same way—so who am I to try and pass judgment on them?"

Paul Jacobs didn't have a friendly smile on his face. We walked along, Mr. Jacobs frowning and tilting his head, first to one side then the other. Mrs. Jacobs watched the ground at her feet. Mama looked down, too. Even from behind her, I could sense the startled, worried look on her face.

It wasn't long before Mr. Jacobs started talking again. Only this time it was about pineapples and the plantation. The conversation didn't get much deeper than that all through dinner.

After we ate, Ted and I went out and threw his base-ball around. He hardly said two words all the time we were out there. It was enough to drive me nuts.

I was sure glad when Mama and Daddy came out. We said our good-byes and headed home.

Our house was at the far end of the block from the Jacobses'. Mama waited until we were out of earshot. "You really think it was your place to tell Mr. Jacobs off about religion?" she asked softly. "He is your boss. What if you get fired?"

"Don't matter," Daddy huffed. At the front porch, he didn't huff—he let out a long sigh. "Maybe I was out of line. Only . . . well . . . Paul Jacobs seems a lot different toward us than he does toward the other people on the island. He treats some of the workers like dirt—always yelling at them and telling them how lazy and worthless they are.

"Maybe I did get a little carried away. But calling people heathens or no accounts, just 'cause they don't believe the exact same way as you do. Well . . . it just hit me wrong. Just went all over me. Sorry."

The second week, things went pretty much like the first. Mama worked at the Lanai City Mercantile with Carmine Jacobs. They visited some, but mostly Mrs. Jacobs spent her time in the back room working on her books.

Daddy didn't have any more run-ins with Mr. Ja-cobs. He worked in the pineapple fields (usually wearing three pairs of pants when he left home in-

stead of two) and he got to be right good friends with
José de los Santos, who was Robert's dad.

I worked hard at school and did my lessons. Mama
always came home to fix lunch and I spent my time
eating slow, instead of rushing back. There just wasn't
a whole lot to do if I got back early. I could watch Ted
throw a baseball on the roof and catch it when it
rolled down. I could watch the girls playing with the
cardboard lids from milk bottles. They called them
pogs and tried to flip them into a little circle drawn in
the dirt—kind of like tiddlywinks. Or, if I wanted
some real excitement, I could watch the guys disap-
pear when I walked toward where they were playing.
Robert de los Santos talked to me a little. But it was
still like pulling teeth to get him to hold still long
enough to visit.

The next Sunday, after church, we didn't eat dinner with the Jacobses. After services, Daddy took the
long way home. He walked Mama and me to the
pineapple field at the edge of town.

It was kind of funny—we'd been on the little island
of Lanai for over two weeks and it was the first time I
got a close look at a pineapple. From a distance, the
fields looked lush and green, like spring wheat back
in Oklahoma. Up close, the things were totally different.

The plants came up in a bunch from the ground.
The leaves, some over a foot long, spread out from
the base, and the leaves' ends were as stiff and sharp
as daggers. The pineapple itself sat right in the middle of the plant. The fruit was kind of an orangish yel-

low, and the top of it had sharp, spiked leaves, too. Even with three pairs of pants on, it was little wonder Daddy came home with his legs all chewed up.

Soon as we got back to the house, Mama made Daddy strip down to his boxers. All week she'd kept zinc ointment on his cuts and scratches. They looked a lot better. Still, there were a couple of new ones.

We'd just settled on the couch to listen to the Honolulu radio station, when all of a sudden, Daddy sat straight up and slapped his leg. Judging by the way his face wrinkled up and he jerked, I guess he plumb forgot about all the cuts and scratches. He eased his hand away and looked down at his leg. He gave a little sigh of relief when he didn't see any blood. Then he turned to me.

"I ran onto Mr. Munro yesterday morning, John," he said, still inspecting his hurt leg. "He needed to talk with you about something. I promised him that I'd send you over. I just flat forgot."

"Is he really loony as a bedbug?" I asked, remembering Mr. Jacobs's words, our first day on the island.

Daddy slapped a hand to his forehead. He rocked back on the couch and squinted at me. Finally, his look softened.

"Mr. Jacobs is friendly. That don't mean he's right all the time."

Chapter 9

Even at fourteen, it's still kind of funny how "little kid" thoughts still hang around in a fella's head. What if this Munro guy really was loony as a bedbug?

I pushed the thoughts aside and mustered my courage. Even so, my hand trembled a bit when I rapped on Munro's front door. What did he want to talk to me about, anyhow?

There was no answer, so I knocked again.

Still nothing.

I knocked one last time. Soon as I did, I froze. I held my breath, listening. A sound came to my ears. It was a faint, tapping sound.

Only the sound didn't come from inside the house. It came from behind me. I turned. A little ways in front of the house was a patch of red gravel. Just beyond that was a little footpath. It wound across a small hump and disappeared at the edge of a valley. Squinting, keeping my ears on the direction of the noise, I followed the little path.

At the edge of the valley, I stopped. Below me was a green field with tall lush grass. A little shed stood at one side, and a wooden corral surrounded most of the field. There were two horses. The sorrel that Carol gave me grazed out in the middle of the pasture. The other, a white horse, stood not far from the shed. I could see a man, on the other side of the fence.

The man was short and pudgy. The white horse kept leaning over the fence to nuzzle him. I couldn't help but notice that the man's hair was almost the same color as the horse. He glanced up when I got near. With a smile, he nodded at the end of the board he was hammering on.

"Latch onto that board there, son."

I got hold of the board and lifted. When it was in the right spot, he drove a nail through it and into a post. Then he came down and pounded a couple of nails into the end I was holding.

Once that was done, he set the hammer on top of the fence post and offered his hand.

"I'm George Munro." He smiled. "You must be John Priddle."

I shook his hand. I couldn't help smiling back at his pleasant grin.

"Yes sir."

"Pleasure to meet you, John. Been meaning to speak with you, but never found the time before. I'm a bit curious about something."

"What's that?" I asked.

"Ginger." He nodded toward the sorrel horse in the middle of the pasture. "She's a right fine little mare. But in the time you been here, you haven't once come by to see her, much less ride her. I was just curious as to why."

It was a little hard to explain how I felt and why I hadn't been over to see the horse. But Mr. Munro seemed easy to talk to. We walked around the outside of the pasture, fixing loose boards and just visiting. Before long, I felt as easy as if he was an old friend.

I explained how guilty I felt about taking the girl's horse and how rotten it was that she had to walk all the way to school. I told him as how I loved horses, but just didn't feel right about riding Ginger and didn't know what to do.

"I can understand how you feel," he admitted. "Giving a gift when someone expresses appreciation is an old custom of the Hawaiian people. A gift as extravagant as a horse—is—a mite much. I found out that Kalola had insulted a visitor to their home and . . ."

"Excuse me, sir," I interrupted. "Who's Ka . . . Kal . . . KaWho?"

"Kalola—Carol." He smiled. "Kalola is her real name, her Hawaiian name. The English version or translation is 'Carol.' Anyway, she had a spat or argument with a visitor and her grandfather was quite put out with her. I think she was trying to make up for what she'd done by showing him that she *did* remember the old traditions. She got a *bit* carried away though, I'll admit. But the bottom line is, want her or not, that little mare's yours. You need to take care of her."

I shook my head and looked down at my Keds.

"I'm sorry, Mr. Munro. I been meaning to start on a pen for her. I sure as heck didn't plan to leave her stuck on you. It's just . . . well . . . just feeling guilty and all about taking her from Carol . . . well, pushing it out of my mind was about the only thing I could do. I just didn't even think about it. But I'll start on my own pen . . ."

"No!" Mr. Munro shook his head, cutting me off. "That isn't it at all, John. Building a pen isn't what I mean." He made a sweeping motion with his hand. "Pasture here has more grass than those two horses could eat in a year. And that's the problem. Little mare of yours is getting fat as a pumpkin. You don't ride her and get her some exercise . . . shoot, she might blow up."

I promised I'd ride Ginger.

With a jerk of his head, he motioned toward the little shed. He put his hammer and nails away, climbed to the top rail, and sat. When he patted the wood rail, I hopped up beside him.

"Anyway, when I found out about Kalola," he went on, "about her giving you the horse . . . well, I been riding down every morning and giving her a lift up the mountain. Ride back through town about the time school's letting out and make sure she gets home okay."

Suddenly I felt like a great weight had been lifted off my shoulders. "That's wonderful!" I yelped.

Mr. Munro leaned back, sort of looking out the corner of one eye at me. "Well, John, we do have us a bit of a problem, though."

Something about his look kind of yanked the smile off my face.

"Got to make a trip to the big island. Pick up building supplies and visit friends. Be gone for a couple of weeks. I won't be around to give Kalola a ride to school and back. Since you're gonna be riding Ginger, anyway, I was hoping you might . . ."

You talk about "Out of the frying pan, into the fire"!

Suddenly I felt trapped like a rat. If Mr. Munro was crazy, it was what Grandma would call "crazy like a fox." That meant somebody who acted loony as a bedbug but was downright smart. First off, he got me to promise I'd ride the horse. The next thing—before I even knew what was happening to me . . . Yep! Trapped like a rat.

"But . . . but . . ." I stammered. "She's a girl."

Mr. Munro's mouth kind of dropped open. His forehead scrunched down as he studied me. Then a sly little smile curved the corners of his mouth.

"What are you, John, thirteen? Fourteen?"

"I'm fourteen."

His eyes kind of rolled up toward the sky.

"Well, your feelings about girls will change soon enough, I suspect." He seemed to be talking more to himself than to me. "In the meantime, I'd consider it a personal favor if you'd . . .

"But, she's a girl," I whined, cutting him off once more. "Two whole weeks . . . a girl . . ."

"She's sure enough a girl." He nodded. "But even girls are human beings. Try to look at it more as doing a favor for a friend—another human being."

Chapter 10

When Daddy and I were alone in the living room, I asked him if he'd wake me up in the morning when he left for work. I didn't want to say one single word to anybody about it, but after considerable thought, I realized I hardly ever got up on my own. So, knowing Daddy usually left an hour or so before Mama got me up for school . . .

When he wanted to know why, I told him about talking to Mr. Munro and how "my new horse" was getting fat and needed exercise. I told him I'd ride her an hour before school and an hour after.

I didn't lie to him. I just didn't tell him everything. The horse did need riding. I promised Mr. Munro that I'd give her some exercise. Only, with the memory of Susie Potter in the back of my mind . . . well, parents don't need to know EVERYTHING.

I got out of bed and dressed, just fine. In the twilight of morning, I walked past Mr. Munro's house and down into the valley where the horse lot and

Ginger were, just fine. I had to chase her around the
lot a couple of times before I finally got her cornered
so I could get the bridle on her. Then I got the blanket and saddle. Everything went—just fine . . .

Until I was about halfway down the hill.

The closer I got to the ocean, the beach, the place
where I was supposed to find Carol's house, the more
I wanted to turn back and just forget the whole thing.
Somebody was bound to see us riding together. Being
a girl, she'd probably hang on around my waist. She'd
probably squeal or try to act scared if the horse trotted
or stumbled or anything like that—just like cousin
Molly back home. She'd probably talk about dresses
and cooking and doing the laundry and all that other
stupid girl stuff.

I sure didn't want no girl touching me or hanging
on around my middle. I hated the thought of all that
giggling and squealing in my ear. It was almost more
than I could bear. Still, I gave my word. I shook my
head, thinking what a crafty old fox that Mr. Munro
guy was.

Ginger and I followed the road down to the little
dock where Captain Sanches had brought me and my
parents, our first day here. From there, I went back
up the hill a little ways to the spot where I had gotten
stuck with this stupid horse by that dumb girl.

Although I couldn't remember the word she'd
said, I remember it meant "toward the ocean," so I
looked at the little ridge where she'd pointed. I

nudged Ginger with my heels. She seemed to know the way better than I did. I let her have her head, and she trotted down to the sandy beach. We followed it around the half-moon shape of the little bay.

The house was nothing like what I expected. It didn't even look like the houses in Lanai City. Fact was, it was different from any house I ever saw. There was no wood on it. The whole thing was made of leaves. They were kind of pointy-like, sort of resembling the pineapple leaves. Only these leaves were long and flat, instead of short and bunchy, like those around a pineapple. The leaves were brown, too, instead of green. The sides, the roof—everything was covered with the long, brown leaves.

When we got closer, I could see there was a wooden porch with a rail around it and beams to hold up the overhang of the roof. I pulled Ginger to a stop, just short of the wooden steps that led to the porch.

"Anybody home?" I called.

There was no answer. Ginger pawed the ground and snorted.

"Carol? You in there? Anybody in there?"

I leaned down alongside Ginger's neck. There was a big room, sort of a living-room thing. On the left side was an old and weathered table with four chairs around it. I couldn't see what was on the right. Behind that room, there were two other rooms. Only I couldn't see inside 'cause there was a blanket hanging in front of each, sort of like a door.

That was it.

That was the whole, entire house. One big room and two little ones.

"Hello!" I called as loud as I could.

"Aloha," a voice called back. It was faint and distant. I couldn't tell where it had come from. I held my breath, listening. Waited for the voice to come again.

"Aloha." The voice came from someplace behind the shack. I tugged on the reins and moved Ginger around the side of the little grass cabin.

There was a field behind the house. It was low and flat and the plants that grew there had these HUGE leaves that were bigger than both of my hands put together. At the far end of the field was an old man.

Even from this distance, I could tell he was old. He wore nothing but khaki pants, rolled up to his knees. Probably old as the island itself, the man was wrinkled and frail. Folds of skin hung loose where once strong muscles had bulged. As I rode closer I could see the brown skin of his face. It was craggy and cracked like old boot leather and his callused hands looked as rough as the lava rock that covered Lanai.

"My name's John Priddle." I announced. "I come to see if Carol wanted a ride to school. Are you her grandpa?"

The old man's brow furrowed. He frowned for just an instant, then smiled.

"I am Kalola's makua. Kalola's parent. I am Makalii Pukui." He reached up and shook my hand. "Come inside and join me for some poi. Rest, drink."

Without being too obvious, I kind of wiggled my

hand from his grasp and cleared my throat. "I'd really like to, but I got to get to school. Is Carol here?"

The old man sighed and cast his eyes from mine.

"My child is most impatient and always *huhu*." He glanced up at me. "*Huhu* mean 'mad' or 'angry'," he explained. "George Munro tell her John Priddle not too happy, but come for her. Kalola say John Priddle like all other haole and not keep word. I am most ashamed for her. She already start to school."

I frowned down at him and shook my head.

"I didn't see her on the road. How long ago . . ."

"She take path *mauka* . . ."

"Huh? Excuse me. What did you say?"

The old man gave a sheepish smile.

"Path there." He pointed toward the mountain. "It is short cut."

"Maybe I can catch her."

"You sure you not stay to rest a moment? Eat something? Maybe drink?"

I smiled back over my shoulder at him. "Thanks, but no thanks. I gave my word to Mr. Munro that I'd fetch her up the hill. And that's what I aim to do."

Sometimes, other folks make it right hard on a fella to keep his word.

Chapter 11

Ginger knew the trail. She went straight to it, and we made pretty good time, trotting up the hill toward Lanai City. Still, Carol was nearly halfway to school before we caught up to her.

We topped a little ridge and spotted her on a flat stretch about fifty yards ahead.

"Hey, Carol!" I called. "Wait up."

She stopped. Her long black hair whipped around her shoulders when she spun to look back. She paused for only a second, then turned and started walking again.

I dug my heels into the little mare's sides and we galloped to get beside her.

"Wait up," I repeated. "I'm supposed to give you a ride to school."

"There is no need," she said without glancing up. "We *kamaaina* do just fine without you haoles."

"What?" I frowned at the back of her head.

She ignored me and kept walking.

"What did you say?"

Still nothing but the back of her head. I kicked

Ginger. She leaped so quickly that I had to hang onto the saddle horn to keep from sliding over her rump. I figured the girl would stop, with us blocking her path. Instead, she just moved to the side and kept walking.

Again, I kicked Ginger. This time, when we got in front of her, I jumped down. I kind of held my arms out, blocking Carol's path like I would a wild heifer's in the calf pen back home.

"I didn't understand a word you said." I moved from side to side to stop her. Her brown eyes seemed almost black when she glared at me. "I don't know what you got your feathers so ruffled about, neither. All I done was come to give you a ride to school. I promised Mr. Munro I would. Didn't he tell you I was coming?"

"He told me. But he also told me you were not too happy." Her eyes tightened to tiny slits. "You did not want to."

I shrugged.

"Well . . . I wasn't jumping for joy, if that's what you mean, but . . . well . . . I'm here and you're here and the horse is here, so . . . ."

"Haole not like Hawaiian! To haole, Hawaiians are worse than kanaka. Haole are all alike!"

We were quite a ways from the path. Even so, she started around me again. I grabbed her arm.

"Look!" I growled. "I'm getting a little tired of all this name calling. What's all this holy stuff you keep calling me?"

Her angry scowl softened. For just a second, I thought she might even smile. Instead, she tried to yank her arm from my grasp. I squeezed tighter. She winced.

"*Haole* means white guy!"

There was something about the way she said "white guy" that made the word sound more like "cowpatty" or "dirtball" instead of "white guy." I didn't like the sound of it—*not at all.*

"I'm not a white guy." I hesitated a moment, then glanced down at my pale hand against her bronze arm. "Okay, so maybe I am white. But I'm not . . . I mean, I'm ah . . ." I let go of her and folded my arms. "Okay, so I'm white. But what's that got to do with anything?"

Her mouth kind of opened a bit, like she was fixing to say something. Then with a sigh, she moved off toward the path. I trotted behind her.

"Look, I don't know what this holy stuff or white guy and Hawaiian stuff is all about. The reason I wasn't too crazy about giving you a ride was 'cause . . ."

She stopped and turned to look at me.

"Well, it's because . . . I . . . er . . ."

I don't know what it was, but it seemed like every time Carol looked at me, I had trouble getting words out of my face.

"Okay, look," I started over again. "One time when I was in second grade, there was this girl named Susie Potter. She and I . . . well, mostly *she* . . . well . . . but, anyhow, we . . ."

* * *

Despite all my sputtering, Carol listened while I told about my experiences with girls. Her expression seemed to soften, but I could tell she still didn't trust me—not altogether. Finally, she gave a little shrug and halfway smiled at me.

"I will accept your offer to ride with you. We will put Ginger in Mr. Munro's lot. It is away from town, so no one will see us. I will wait until you leave, then I will walk to school alone. When school is done, we will walk separate paths. I will wait with Ginger until you come. No one will know."

We had made our way back to the trail. Carol motioned to the saddle and held the reins while I got on. She gave the horse a loving pat on her nose, then handed me the reins and backed up a couple of steps.

"And if being a girl is what really troubles you," she said as she reached up her hand to me. "I will not be a girl while I am with you."

With that, she grabbed my forearm. I pulled and she gave a little leap. Light as a feather, she landed behind the saddle.

I was impressed.

Carol didn't wrap herself around my middle, either. She held to the cantle. Fact was, except for a little puff of wind, now and then that blew strands of her long, black hair forward to brush against my ear or cheek, I would have never known she was there.

Like I said, I was impressed. Still, what she'd said about not being a girl . . . I glanced over my shoulder.

"What did you mean when you said you wouldn't

be a girl when you're with me? Way I see it, there ain't much way you can hide that."

She leaned forward, beside me. From the corner of my eye I could see her smile.

"I cannot change what I am," she admitted. "But there is more than what you see."

I frowned.

"Like . . . ?"

"Like fishing. Is there fishing where you come from—in Oklahoma?"

"Well, sure. Fishing and hunting both."

"And is that what boys speak of, when they are together?"

"Yeah. I reckon."

"It is much the same here. When friends come to visit my grandfather, there is always talk about fishing. Makalii Pukui is best fisherman in all of Hawaii. Kalola Pukui is next best."

A little cough slipped out when I turned back to watch the path.

"Yeah . . . I bet."

"You bet," she repeated. "Did John Priddle ever catch big fish?"

"Sure," I answered confidently. "Landed this catfish one time at Whitener's Pond. Thing woulda gone eight pounds. Maybe ten."

Carol laughed. I yanked on the reins and made Ginger stop so I could turn around in the saddle and glare at the girl behind me.

"Suppose you caught a bigger one. Suppose

you caught a fish what weighed twelve pounds, right?"

She clamped her lips closed to keep from laughing. She tried to look serious when she shook her head.

"I did not ask if you use big *bait* to catch fish. I asked if you ever caught a big fish."

"Huh?" I frowned.

"*Ulua* runs maybe thirty to forty pounds. *Ahi* much bigger. Your fish would not even make good bait for *ahi*."

"How much bigger?" I frowned.

"Bigger."

"You ever catch one?"

Carol shrugged. "Many."

"What was the biggest?"

Thinking, she kind of sucked one side of her bottom lip into her mouth and nibbled on it.

"Don't know how much the biggest weighed. Three summers ago, I caught one off Kaunolu. Big ahi. Good fighter. Dragged us almost to Lahaina Town before we got him in the boat. Grandfather said that since we were so close to the docks, we might as well go weigh him."

"And?"

Carol shrugged.

"Good fish. Scales at Lahaina Town said one hundred eighty-six pounds."

Chapter 12

Now, I'd been around enough fishermen to know that slight exaggerations sometimes occur. When one fisherman's talking to another, well . . . there's some kind of unseen force that pushes the hands just a little bit farther apart, each time he shows someone how big his fish was. Gravity seems to increase, too— at least by a pound or so—each time the story is told. And the one that got away . . . they're always the world's record. Daddy'd told me, "It ain't lying. It's just fishing."

But a hundred eighty-six pounds! NO WAY!

Came real close to blowing the whole thing that first morning. If Carol hadn't reached around me, taken the reins, and kicked Ginger to get her going . . . well, I guess we would have still been sitting there by the time school was over.

As it was, I slipped through the door just as Mr. Foster came out on the steps to ring the bell. True to her word, Carol came in about five minutes later so that no one would know we had ridden together. I felt kind of guilty about it 'cause Mr. Foster scolded and fussed at her for a good ten minutes on account of being late to class.

She never once said it was my fault for wanting to sit on the hill and argue with her about the size of a fish. Fact was, she never so much as looked in my direction, the whole time Mr. Foster was chewing on her.

Mama had fried chicken and green beans for lunch. I gobbled it down and got back to school as quick as I could.

When I asked Ted Jacobs what an ahi was, he just looked at me. So figuring he didn't know the Hawaiian name, I simply asked him how big the fish were around here.

Ted's nose kinda crinkled up. He rubbed the fingertips and thumbs of both hands together, then flopped his hands back and forth like he was trying to get something nasty off of them.

"I don't like fish," he whined. "They stink."

It was the most talking Ted had done since I'd been here. And it was all I could do to keep my eyes from rolling clean up into the top of my skull.

Robert and a Japanese boy named Shintaro were over with the other boys, choosing up sides for a baseball game. As always, when I walked up, everybody left. Pretending they were doing something else, talking, starting a different game—whatever—it was always the same. This time I didn't let it bother me.

"Robert," I called when he started away from me. "Do you know what an ahi is?"

He smiled politely. "It's a fish. What you call a tuna."

"They big?"

"I guess." He shrugged.

"How big?"

Shintaro stepped up beside him. "I have not to catch one. But see them in boats one time. They maybe long as Shin." He pointed to himself. "Weigh more. Maybe much as Shin's papa."

My mouth flopped open and I felt a rush of cool air fill my lungs. Maybe Carol wasn't lying. Maybe . . .

Before I could say anything else, both boys turned and slipped away.

Somehow . . . some way . . . Carol did just like she said she would. She *wasn't* a girl when she was with me.

On the rides to and from school, we talked about fishing and hunting and stuff like that. I told her about shooting quail with my grandpa's shotgun or hunting rabbits with a .22 rifle. Carol said that she had never been hunting, but the boys hunted pig. They used spears, just like they did when hunting *honu*. She had speared honu before.

I found out that a honu was a green sea turtle. But even after listening to Carol's description and stories, I still couldn't imagine how or why anyone would have to use a spear to catch a dumb, slow old turtle. She promised to show me some day.

Every morning, when Ginger and I picked Carol up for the ride to school, Mr. Pukui would ask me in to eat some poi or sit and rest.

Carol explained that it was a custom to invite people to eat and drink. She said that even a stranger should not pass somebody's house without being invited, and she hinted that it would be impolite for me to keep refusing.

She also explained that her name was Kalola. At school, Mr. Foster made her use her "American" name. But her real name—her Hawaiian name—was Kalola.

Friday, after school, instead of taking her straight home, we rode the opposite direction. We kept the ridge of the mountain to our right. She wouldn't tell me where we were going, but it was a good ride. We kept Ginger at a fast trot. As we rode, I couldn't help but notice the trees. Carol—I mean, Kalola—she told me they were Norfolk Pines. Mr. Munro and his wife had lived on Lanai since they were first married. For many years, he had carried the pine seeds in his saddle bags and planted the trees.

It was a long ride, but we finally stopped at the weirdest place I ever saw in my life. It was kind of a field on the top of a hill. Only, instead of a field of pineapple or little pine saplings, or even a field of cactus and scrub mesquite trees, this field was full of rock.

There were boulders all over the place. Huge boulders, small ones, just scattered around in the red, rocky dirt. Even coming from Oklahoma, I'd seen boulders before. About a two-hour drive from our farm was a place called the Wichita Mountains. Back when Grandpa and Betty were both alive, we'd take the Model T and drive down once or twice a year. There were boulders all over the Wichitas. Besides, my parents and I had taken the train through the Rockies to get to San Francisco. There were *big* boulders in the Rocky Mountains.

The thing about the Wichitas and the Rockies—well, the boulders were always down near the bottom of a mountain. Cluttered or clumped around where they'd fallen and rolled down or something.

Here, at this place, there was nowhere for them to roll down from. The rocks were on the very top with absolutely nothing else around.

"It is called the Garden of the Gods," she explained when she got down from Ginger.

"Where did all the big rocks come from?" I asked, still looking around for a place they might have rolled down.

"Pele threw them."

"Who's Pele?" I swung down from the saddle.

"Pele is the goddess of fire—of the volcano. She once lived in Palawai." She pointed. "The basin where Lanai City and the pineapple fields are. She now lives in Kilauea, on the big island."

I frowned and followed her through the field of enormous boulders.

"You believe in gods and goddesses?"

She stopped and turned to face me. I couldn't help smiling back when she smiled. "No. I believe in one God and in Jesus. But Makalii still believes. I like to listen to his stories. He said Pele is a very angry goddess. In her anger she made all the islands."

"All the islands?" I frowned. "You mean this one and the one where Honolulu is."

"No. All the islands."

"There's more than two?"

She turned to look at me. "There are many. Don't you know this?"

I shrugged and shook my head.

"Monday, after school, we will ride to Lanaihale. I will show you."

We walked and looked around. Long, black shadows crawled from the rocks. It was eerie—almost spooky—the way the place made me feel.

All of a sudden, I noticed I was alone. I stopped dead in my tracks, and looked around. Kalola was no place in sight. I called out to her a couple of times. When she didn't answer, I started hunting.

Between the eerie surroundings and the quiet, it might near scared me to death when she jumped out from behind a big rock and yelled.

I spun, glaring at her through tight eyes. She only laughed.

"You scared the devil outa me," I snarled. She laughed again. I doubled up my fist and punched her on the arm.

Darned if she didn't slug me back. She had a right hook every bit as good as Charlie Eagle's. If I hadn't blocked it with my shoulder, it probably would have knocked the wind out of me.

We scuffled around awhile, then took turns playing hide and seek. We talked all the way home, and I could hardly wait for Monday.

Chapter 13

"The trees are called Norfolk Pines. Mr. Munro planted most of 'em himself. He was the foreman of the Baldwin Cattle Ranch. The ranch was here before Mr. Dole bought Lanai. The cattle and sheep overgrazed this island, so Mr. Munro rides around and plants trees. There's other islands all around us. I seen 'em. Just this afternoon. Maui is the other side of the mountain."

I talked fast, like if I slowed down I'd forget something or not have time to get it all in.

"And there's a little horseshoe island called Molokini, and lots of fish live in the middle of it; then there's a flat island, only, I can't remember the name, and Hawaii must be huge 'cause it's got mountains that are so high there's snow on them all the time." I stopped and sucked in a breath. Then I pointed out the back door. "Over that way is Molokai. There's leopards there on one side of the island, so not many people go there. Only, all around it is some of the best fishing in the whole, entire world. Great big fish! Some are as big as Ginger. Can you imagine a fish that big? And there's boats going back and forth to Maui all the time 'cause folks here got relatives that live over there. Besides, it's only eight miles across the channel. Right here on this island . . ." I had to stop again to catch my breath.

"I think it's lepers, instead of leopards," Mama corrected when I stopped to breathe. "Carmine mentioned something about a leper colony on Molokai. The people there have a bad disease, so they have to be isolated from other people."

I was a bit disappointed that there weren't any leopards. One day I had hoped Carol and I could go and see one. Still, that didn't dampen my excitement.

"Well, anyway," I went right on. "There's a place, right here on Lanai, called Garden of the Gods. I went there, Friday. There's all these big rocks and stuff. Nothing else. No plants or grass or nothing— just rocks. Tomorrow, we're going to a place called Shipwreck Beach. It's on the far side of the island, so it might be dark 'fore I get home. Then Wednesday . . ."

Mama was cooking fried taters 'n' onions in the big black skillet. She stuck the scoop under the middle and turned them over.

"Where'd you get all this information about the other islands?" she asked.

Daddy stood on the other side of her. "And you keep saying, 'we.' Who's this 'we' you keep talking about?" He waited a second for the sizzling sound to stop, then he snuck him a bite from the skillet.

I was just reaching from the other side to swipe

some taters 'n' onions, too. Only, when Mama asked who I was getting all my information from, and Daddy heard me saying "we," instead of "I," my hand froze in mid-reach. My mouth kind of fell open.

Now you've done it, I thought. *Now they're gonna know you been paling around with a girl. They're gonna start in on that girlfriend bit.*

I blinked a couple of times and got my eyes shrunk back down so they weren't as big around as the skillet. Then I cleared my throat and took a deep breath.

"It's a friend . . ." I cleared my throat again. "A friend from school."

"I'm glad you finally got a friend," Daddy said, snitching another handful from Mama's skillet. "You didn't say much, but I had the feeling you weren't too happy at school."

Mama shot him a look for stealing food. But I guess she caught the movement from my hand in the skillet, 'cause she turned on me.

"Who is this friend?" She squinted at the handful of taters. "What's his name? What's he like?"

Lucky for me, I'd already popped my stolen taters 'n' onions into my mouth. I always reached for the crispy brown clumps that were stuck together. There's nothing tastier than fried taters 'n' onions, right out of the skillet. The time it took to keep them from burning my tongue and to get them chewed . . . well, it gave me time to think.

"Name's Kalola," I answered. I felt real sly about re-membering Carol's Hawaiian name. Mama and

Daddy knew that Carol was a girl's name. They probably didn't have any idea about Kalola.

"Kalola," Mama repeated. "Strange sort of name. Where's he from?"

"Ah . . . ah, right here."

Daddy peeked around her from the other side and kind of sneered at me.

"Everybody's from right here." He swiped more taters 'n' onions. "I mean where did he come from? Is he Filipino or Japanese or . . ."

Mama raised her wood turner, threatening him. While her attention was on Daddy, I reached in and swiped me another brown clump.

"From Hawaii. From Lanai."

Still munching his stolen goodies, Daddy leaned forward and propped his elbow on the edge of the stove. He rested his cheek against his fist.

"I thought most of the Hawaiians lived on the other side of the island." He frowned. "They even have their own school over in a little place called Keomuku. I didn't know there were any Hawaiians over on this side of Lanai."

"Oh sure," I said. A sharp, crusty tater edge jabbed against the side of my throat when I swallowed. "Remember that little girl who gave me the horse? She lives over here. Remember?"

"The Pukuis?" Daddy's frown grew deeper. "I remember meeting the old man, the day Paul Jacobs took me down there with him to see if he wanted to sell his place. Don't remember stopping at any other place on this side of the island." Thinking, remembering, his brow was really scrunched down now. "Don't recall seeing any boy, though. Just that girl. They related?"

"Ah . . . ah . . . yeah, I guess you could say that."

"Well, where's the house?"

It was Daddy's hungries and Mama who saved me. So far, I'd managed to answer all his questions without really lying to him. Now I was stuck. Only, when Daddy reached for another handful of tater 'n' onions, Mama had had enough.

She whopped the back of his hand with her wood turner. Then, sure he was out of her skillet, she turned on me.

"That's enough! Both of you. We'll not have any for supper if you two keep snitching all the food. Now both of you, *scat*!"

I scurried out on the front porch. That was a close call. I figured Daddy would sit down on the couch and listen to the radio until supper was ready. He didn't. He followed me out onto the porch.

My teeth ground together inside my head. He was either gonna make me tell him I been spending my time with a girl . . . or he was gonna make me lie to him. I didn't know which.

"You say that Mr. Munro had been foreman of a cattle ranch?"

"Yes, sir."

I knew I was safe when he got that far off look in his eye. I'd seen the look before—usually when he was working on one of his inventions or tinkering with something. Whatever he was thinking about, it wasn't Kalola Pukui. He looked up at the sky.

"Hmmm ... ranch foreman ... cowboy ... hmmm."

Daddy didn't eat much supper. He kept staring off at the walls or the ceiling, thinking, that faraway look in his eyes.

After dinner, Mama made him take his overalls off. Nobody came to Mama's table with their clothes off. Even in the dead of August back home, we had to wear a shirt and everything. But she needed to get the zinc ointment on his legs and didn't want his overalls rubbing it off. Ever since he started working with the pineapples, once supper was over, Daddy sat around in his boxers.

All at once, he sort of jerked. He gave a little blink and looked straight at me.

"You been riding the horse every day, right?"

I cringed. "Yes, sir." Here we go again. He's gonna ask me about Kalola.

"Saddle and bridle out of Mr. Munro's shed?"

"Yes, sir."

"See any chaps hanging in there?"

I frowned, thinking. "Don't remember seeing any."

Suddenly Daddy was on his feet.

"He was a ranch foreman." Daddy smiled. "I bet money he's got some chaps."

Daddy took off for the back door. Mama hopped up and took off after him.

"Keith? Keith! For gosh sakes, put some pants on!"

Chapter 14

I thought the Garden of the Gods was weird, but Daddy had it beat. He was the weirdest-looking thing I ever saw in my life.

He stood in the middle of the living room in his boxer shorts. Around his middle he had on a pair of thick, leather chaps with his bare legs sticking out.

Even though it was dark outside, Mama was a bit embarrassed that he'd been out running around in his underwear. She couldn't believe he'd run down to Mr. Munro's barn, with nothing on but his shorts and a work shirt. Still, neither of us could keep from laughing. The harder we tried not to, the worse it got. I ended up rolling on the couch, holding my belly. Mama ended up sitting on the floor.

Daddy just stood and looked at us. He tried to act disgusted, only I could see the little sparkle in his eye.

"Don't care how silly it looks," he sneered. "If they work, it's worth it."

Way that Daddy explained it, some of the men wore three or four pairs of pants or overalls when they picked the pineapples. He said some of them were layered and packed in so tight that it looked like their eyes were gonna pop clean out of their heads every time they bent over. Tomorrow, he'd put on one pair of overalls with the thick leather chaps over them. If they worked, he'd get Paul Jacobs to call Mr. Munro. Have him stop by the Parker Ranch, before he left the big island and bring back enough for Daddy's and José de los Santos's whole crew.

It sounded like a right smart idea. Still, looking at him standing there with his white, skinny legs sticking out from under them cowboy chaps, I couldn't keep from laughing.

Carol—I mean, Kalola—she laughed, too, when I described him to her on the ride to school Wednesday morning. Then I asked if her parents had ever done stupid stuff like my daddy did.

"My parents are dead."

That's all she said.

It made me feel bad. I mean, I knew she lived with her grandfather. I should have figured something had happened to her parents. Only, I just didn't think.

I kept feeling worse all through the day. At noon, she didn't join the other girls for their pog game. She sat alone on the swings. Tatsu, Shintaro's little sister, sat with her for a time. They talked, but I could tell Kalola's mind was a million miles from the playground.

I wanted to tell her how sorry I was for saying something that reminded her about her parents. I wanted to let her know that I understood. Not just that I was sorry, but that I *really* understood what it was like to lose somebody.

There were other kids on the playground. And with other people about, I couldn't!

So I spent the rest of recess standing around—just as alone as she was—watching Ted Jacobs throw the ball on the roof and catch it when it rolled down.

Shipwreck Beach was kind of neat. We crossed the hump—that's what Kalola called the top of the island—and followed a dirt road down toward the sea. The road turned to the right, only we went left. There was a sandy beach there and some big chunks of wood lying all over the place. We left Ginger grazing on one of the sand dunes and walked around for a closer look.

The chunks of wood were boards. At one time they had been cut and sanded smooth. Now they were pitted and scarred by the wind and sand that swept across the beach. We found what looked like the old hull of a ship. Some of its wood was so thick that I couldn't even get my hand around the end of it. We climbed and pretended we were sailors on a whaling ship or something. Kalola said there were other wrecks along the beach, but it was getting late so we didn't have time to play or explore.

*   *   *

It was hard to ignore how quiet my friend was on the ride back home.

"I'm sorry I said something about your mom and dad," I apologized. "I didn't mean to bring it up. I didn't know it was gonna hurt you so much."

"It is okay." She patted me on the shoulder. "I was a little girl when they died. I don't remember them too well. Not remembering them made me hurt inside."

With my weight in one stirrup, I twisted around in the saddle so I could look at her.

"They get sick or something?"

"No. A fishing accident."

There was something in the way she said, "fishing accident," that bothered me. Something that let me know she was hiding something—not telling me all there was to tell. At the same time, I didn't want to hurt her again, so I let it slide.

We rode quiet for a time. Ginger plodded along at a nice, steady pace. She seemed to know the path. I put my weight in one stirrup again. Only this time, instead of just turning my head around, I lifted my weight with my hands, dragged one leg across the seat, and ended up sitting backwards in the saddle.

Kalola looked a little startled. Guess she'd never seen anyone ride backwards. Only, for some reason, I just had to be facing her—looking her square in the eye.

"I had a little sister, once," I began. "Her name was Betty. Had a grandfather, too. Don't think I much wanted a little sister, not at first. All she did was cry and wet her diapers. Then, when she got a little bigger and started walking and stuff, she was all the time getting into my toys. I didn't like her much then, either.

"Only, she kept getting bigger and sort of got to be fun. We played chase and laughed. I loved to listen to her giggle. She gave me little hugs and stuff—all the time. Full of devilment and just cute as a bug. She was so alive and full of life, then the next minute she was dead. I . . . I never knew how much I could miss her. Not until she was gone."

I dropped Kalola off at her home, and I was nearly halfway up the hill when it hit me.

Kalola Pukui was my best friend. We'd really only known each other for two weeks. Still, we were best friends.

Charlie Eagle was my best friend. He knew about Betty and Grandpa. Like most neighbors, he knew how they both come down with what the doctor called rheumatic fever—both on the very same day. He knew the doctor had given them medicine, but warned us that there wasn't much else he could do. And Charlie knew that Grandpa died and two days later Betty passed away. All our neighbors knew that. Most all of them came to the funeral.

But I'd never even told Charlie how much I missed them—especially Betty. I never told him how much it hurt inside and how unfair it was and how I got mad at God and got to feeling sorry for myself and cried myself to sleep a bunch at night. I never told none of that to anybody—not even my best friend. And I never—never ever—cried in front of him.

Even if she was a girl (and I hardly ever thought of Kalola that way), but even if she was, she was still the best, best friend a guy could ever have.

Chapter 15

"Some friend you are!" I snarled.

Carol—Kalola—glared at me across the seat of the saddle. Her big, brown eyes were almost black. She had them scrunched down so tight they were only tiny slits in her face. I jerked the cinch and flipped the leather strap across the saddle. Carol flipped her side—the buckle—across the seat. We stood and glared at each other for a moment more before I yanked the saddle off and hung it in Mr. Munro's shed.

Ginger pitched and bucked as soon as Kalola took her bridle off and let her into the pasture. My "friend" was still glaring at me when she came to hang the bridle over the saddle horn.

"Some friend you are," I repeated. "There ain't no way I'm going out in the ocean in no boat! Every time I get on a boat I end up puking my guts out. Get sick as a dog. I ain't going on no boat! I ain't going out in the ocean! I ain't even getting near the dumb ocean!"

"For two weeks, all John Priddle talks about is catching a big fish. I asked Makalii and he said okay."

She threw her arms up. "Now John Priddle does not want to fish. Wants to throw big baby fit instead."

"I ain't throwing no baby fit. I just didn't know we had to go out on the ocean."

She got a real smart-aleck look on her face and wobbled her head back and forth. "You think fish swim up on bank, and we go pick them up? You think fishing means we dig around in sand to find fish there?"

"No," I sneered back at her. "I just thought there was like a pond or lake or something."

"No lake. No pond. You want fish, go to ocean."

"No way!"

She put her fists on her hips. "Fine! I'll tell grandfather John Priddle is a big sissy and . . ."

I jabbed my hands on my hips.

"Don't you be calling me no sissy."

"Sissy," she sneered.

"I mean it!" My hands drew to fists at my sides.

"Sissy boy."

"Carol, I ain't kidding!"

"Sissy. Sissy. Sissy boy."

My hands flew out against her chest. I shoved as hard as I could. She staggered back a couple of steps, then landed flat on her butt in the dust.

It really surprised me when she bounced right back up. It was like she had springs in her bottom or something. One second she was on the ground and the next, her hands slammed into my chest.

* * *

Guess it's part of being best friends. I spent the whole morning wanting to beat the tar out of her. I hated her guts. By noon I had cooled off. By the time we got back, caught Ginger, and threw the saddle on her . . . well, I guess best friends are like that. One minute, two fellas can be madder than the devil at one another and fighting. The next . . . well . . . you're back to being best friends—just like nothing ever happened. Best friends also let you off the hook when they've bested you.

"Sorry I knocked you down," Kalola said when she swung up behind the saddle.

"It's okay. You didn't push me all that hard," I lied. "Just tripped over a rock or something."

From the corner of my eye, I saw her nod her head and smile.

"Yes. Same rock got me."

By the time we got down the hill, Kalola had me convinced that maybe—just maybe—I could survive being out in the ocean. She said they would stay mostly near the reef. A reef was a shallow place out in the water that broke up the big waves. She also assured me we'd stay close to land. She would have her grandfather bring something she called gingerroot that would help, too. And if I still got sick, after all that, she promised that they would bring me back to the shore.

I made her cross her heart and pinkie-swear. She didn't know what a pinkie-swear was. Not till I showed her. But that's what best friends are for.

Taking her grandfather up on his offer to come "eat some poi, rest, and visit for a while" would be a good idea, too.

"Never talk business around the poi bowl." Kalola went over the "rules" one last time before we got to the house. "Use one, two, or three fingers. Just the tips, don't bury your hand in the poi. Never pull your hand roughly through the poi. Turn the fingers and gently put to your mouth. . . . Do not say 'thank you' when you are finished. . . ."

Eating poi sounded more like a ritual than just sitting down to eat. Kalola went over every single thing I needed to do or not do. She told me everything . . . everything except . . . how nasty poi tasted.

Kind of a pinkish-gray color, it had a texture like school paste—with just about as much flavor. It was all I could do to get it down. And hard as I tried, I couldn't keep my nose from crinkling up.

I don't think Mr. Pukui noticed because he kept right on talking about the weather. Kalola must have seen how much trouble I was having, though. She excused herself, walked to the cabinet, and got down a large bowl. She poured some sugar from it into a smaller bowl made of polished wood.

"I like sugar with my poi, sometimes," she said, bringing the bowl to the table. "It is not the best way to enjoy poi. I hope you do not mind."

Without her grandfather seeing, she glanced toward the sugar bowl and gave a little wink.

"I don't mind," I said, trying not to sound too desperate. "I might even try it that way myself."

I watched as she dipped two fingers into the pinkish, stuff. She touched the gooey mess into the sugar—coating it just a bit—then put it gently to her mouth. I did the same. Only, instead of just a dab of sugar, I coated it all over. It helped.

The poi was still terrible, but at least I could swallow without gagging. I ate it real slow, hoping Kalola and Mr. Pukui would finish most of it off so that I wouldn't have to.

Eating poi was a whole lot like fence hanging. That's what Daddy called it when farmers got together. That's 'cause they'd kind of hang or lean on the fence when they talked about the weather or crops or important stuff like that.

After an eternity, we finished the poi. I almost said "thank you" but caught myself and remembered. Instead, I told him that the poi was very good and I felt rested—now I had to start home.

Mr. Pukui followed us out onto the wooden porch. I untied Ginger's reins and stuck my foot in the stirrup.

"My granddaughter tells me you like fishing," he said.

I nodded quickly. "Yes, sir. I sure do."

"Come tomorrow. We go for ulua. You have goggles?"

I frowned. "What?"

"Goggles. Help Kalola get bait."

I cocked my head to the side and glanced down at Kalola. "What's English for goggles?" I whispered.

Her mouth twitched from side to side. She tilted her head one way, then the other. Like she was thinking on it—really hard.

"Goggles," she answered finally. I couldn't help notice the little twinkle in her eye. She turned to her grandfather.

"John Priddle does not have goggles," she answered for me.

Mr. Pukui walked right up next to Ginger and stared up at me. His leathery, wrinkled brow looked like canyons as he studied my face for a long time. Finally, he smiled.

"We have extra. Take some work, but we fix for him. Maybe fish later."

I guess I was so excited about getting to go fishing, it made the ride back up the hill seem like it took forever.

"I will not be a girl when I am with you."

The memory of her words that first morning on the ride to school crept into my head. Just hearing them inside my skull made my eyes blink. A smile tugged at the corners of my mouth.

Darned if she didn't manage to pull it off, I mused. She really isn't a girl when she's with me. I blinked again. How about that?

The thought of having a best friend who was a girl,

but who really *wasn't* a girl ... well, it got me clear through supper and a long restless night of flipping and flopping in bed. It got me through the ride down the hill to the Pukui house. It got me clean through— up until that moment when I called to let Kalola and her grandfather know I was there, and until she stepped onto the front porch.

Then, all of a sudden ...

There was more GIRL than I ever saw—ever imagined seeing—in my whole, entire life.

Chapter 16

Kalola Pukui was darn-near naked!

I swung down from Ginger and stood, holding the reins. Kalola stepped onto the wooden porch at the front of the leaf-covered shack with nothing on but a couple of strips of bright colored cloth.

When I saw her, my mouth flopped open. The air wouldn't come in and it wouldn't go out. I just stood there with my eyes probably as wide open as my mouth.

"Grandfather is gathering taro root in the garden. He says come and get him when we put Ginger in pen. He will fix your goggles. Here."

I heard her voice, but I don't reckon I heard one single word of what she said. She tossed something to me. I didn't even notice until it thumped against my chest, then dropped to the dirt at my feet. All I noticed was her bare shoulders, and bare tummy, and sides, and back, and legs.

A little strip of cloth went around her top and was tied with a knot in the front. It was a bright yellow material, with purple flowers painted on it. The thing wasn't more than six inches wide. Even less where the knot was.

Another cloth of the same material, covered her down lower. It looked kind of like a diaper—wrapped around her and all tucked in. And when she turned sideways to come down the steps, two little strips of cloth is all there was from the top of her head, clean down to the bottoms of her bare feet. I mean, that was it!

She stood right in front of me and said something, only I didn't hear it. I felt sort of weird. It was kind of like there was a knot, down deep in my stomach and another one up in my throat. And I felt sort of warm or hot around my eyes and face. Kalola frowned and spoke again. Only, I didn't hear her this time, either.

"Huh?" I asked.

Looking disgusted and shaking her head, she leaned down and picked up whatever had dropped at my feet.

"Your goggles," she said, stuffing something into my hand. "Come on."

She took Ginger's reins and headed behind the house. I stood there for what seemed like an eternity. Finally, I blinked a couple of times and looked down. In my hand were a couple of round pieces of wood with glass stuck inside them. A little leather strap joined the two pieces of wood together and two more leather straps stuck out from either side.

I didn't give much thought to what was in my hand, nor look at it too closely. Instead, I followed Kalola. She put Ginger in the pen near the hut. Her grandfather was working in the field. When he saw us, he put his hoe down and came to join us.

"Aloha, John Priddle," he greeted.

I felt the corners of my mouth tug. "Hi." I heard the word, but didn't even realize it came from me. I didn't look at him, either. I couldn't seem to take my eyes off Kalola.

Suddenly Makalii Pukui was between us. I blinked and felt the heat rush to my cheeks. I didn't mean to stare at her, only ... well ... I just couldn't seem to help myself. It didn't embarrass me at all, though. Not until I was staring face-to-face with her grandfather. Suddenly I didn't think I'd ever been so embarrassed in my entire life. My whole face felt like it was on fire, and I could hardly look at the old man.

His smile was gentle, though. He reached down and took the two pieces of wood from my hand. I stared down and didn't look up.

"Need goggles to see inside ocean. Got to fix so they fit face, first. Otherwise, not so good."

He cupped a weathered, wrinkled hand under my chin and lifted my head. Then he put the wood goggles against my face.

Through the glass, I couldn't see a thing but his hand as he held them against my head. He sort of tilted my face from one side to the other.

"Huh," he grunted finally. "Need fixing. Kalola," he called. "Bring long, flat lava rock from kitchen. Probably need stick with sharkskin, too. Bring down to ocean, and we get to work."

I tried not to be too obvious about peeking around

him, trying to see Kalola again. All of a sudden, his eyes were right in front of me.

"You bring ah . . . ah . . ." He turned to Kalola. "What is name for *malo?*"

"Bathing trunks," she smiled, proudly.

"You bring bathing trunks?"

"No, sir." I shook my head. Almost desperate, I turned to Kalola. "You said we was going fishing. You didn't say nothing about swimming."

"Got to get bait before go fish," Mr. Pukui shrugged. "No problem. We make malo. It is old time bathing . . . bathing . . ."

"Trunks." Kalola helped him finish.

"Malo is old time bathing trunks, like I wear when a boy. Not fancy, but work good."

With a jerk of his head, he motioned me to follow him.

I felt like a total idiot! I stood, barefoot in the sand at the edge of the ocean. The wooden goggles wrapped around my head and tied in the back with the leather strap. Goggles, and a piece of cloth, tied with a knot and tucked in all around—kind of like a baby's diaper, only without the pins. Even after Mr. Pukui showed me how to do it about three times, it still took me three or four more tries before I could get it all wrapped and tucked in.

Even at that, I felt like one good sneeze and I would have been buck naked.

The only thing that saved me was the fact that

Kalola was out in the ocean. I could see her head and goggles, every now and then, when she came up for air. She'd take a deep breath, then flip bottom-up and kick her feet to dive down out of sight once more.

Mr. Pukui tugged at the knot where the goggle straps were tied. He forced the goggles so tight, I could feel the edges of the bamboo digging into the sides of my face. He left them on for quite a while, then untied the knot. When they were off, he studied my face, looking for where the goggles had left a mark or dent in my skin. Then he took the flat lava stone and used it like a file to hone down the rough spots.

We must have gone through this process six or seven times. Then he sent me into the ocean, with instructions to get my face under the water. When I came up, I was to put my fingers on any spots where the water leaked in. Hold them there until I got back to him.

While this was going on, Kalola seemed to work her way closer to the shore. She didn't look at me, though. With the goggles on and my fingers marking the spots where it leaked, I didn't look at her either. She'd call out to her grandfather to see if we were done, then go swim some more.

I did this about three or four times. Each time, he would take the goggles and the flat stick that was covered with stuff that looked like sand paper. (He called it sharkskin, but it still looked and felt like sandpaper.) Anyway, he'd rub and file on the spot where I told him it leaked, then have me put them back on and go out into the water.

By the time we were done, the goggles didn't hurt or dig into my face and no water came in—none at all.

"Now can we go fishing, Mr. Pu . . ."

I never got the "kui" part out! Right at that second, Kalola came out of the ocean not far from where we stood. Her bronze skin seemed to glisten in the bright sun. Her long black hair clung to her back and shoulders. And the cloth, now wet from her swim . . . well, it clung to everything else.

"Kalola got rope, hooks, and spear in the outrigger?" Mr. Pukui asked.

Only, she didn't answer him. She stopped a few feet away and looked at me—I guess—just like I was looking at her.

Mr. Pukui said something. Neither one of us heard it. So he spoke again. Once more, we both ignored him.

Suddenly he stepped between us. He raised his right leg and stomped it down hard into the sand. Then he slammed his fist against his chest, making it pop with the deep, thudding sound of a drum.

Startled, both of us looked at him.

"No fish!" His old, weathered face was mad. His soft, gentle voice was a roar. "No find bait! All you do is look at him! All you do is look at her! No look! We go home!"

Chapter 17

There wasn't a darned thing I could say. Mr. Pukui was right. I *had* looked at the girl every chance I could, and I was ashamed of myself for it.

But the way I saw it, he shouldn't be getting onto her. Kalola never once looked at me. I mean, except for that one time when the both of us were standing on the beach—right before the old man blew up. I know, 'cause as many times as I peeked at her, not once was she so much as even looking in my direction.

It just wasn't fair for him to be mad at her for something that was my fault. But for the life of me, I didn't see why she didn't say anything to her grandfather. I mean . . . she hadn't done nothing wrong.

Kalola was already dressed in her long, blue school skirt with the white blouse, when I shoved the blanket aside and came out of Mr. Pukui's bedroom. We walked around the house and headed to the pen where Ginger was. Mr. Pukui went back to his taro field.

We caught Ginger and put her bridle on. I got the saddle and blanket from the little shed and put it on her back. Kalola went to the other side and straightened the girt then passed it under Ginger's belly to me. After I'd tightened the cinch, both of us just stood there. We didn't say anything. We didn't look at each other. We just stood.

Finally, she laced her fingers together over the cantle and rested her chin on her hands. I laced my fingers over the fork and rested my chin on them. Both of us looked at each other for a long time.

"I'm right sorry," I said finally. "I sure didn't mean to get neither of us in trouble. I just . . . I . . . er . . ." I took a deep breath and sighed. "I just never saw a girl before . . . well . . . not dressed like that, I mean. I . . . I'm . . . I'm sure sorry."

"Me too."

I studied her a moment and motioned toward the old man hoeing in the taro field.

"How come you didn't stand up for yourself? I mean, you ought to tell your grandfather that you wasn't looking at me. If you want me to I can tell him for you and . . ."

The look on her face shut me up. I frowned and tilted my head to the side. One side of her mouth tightened to a little smile.

"You mean you were looking?" I gasped.

She nodded.

"But I never saw you. Not once."

The smile crept to the other side of her mouth.

"I know."

We stared at each other until I blinked. Then both of us looked down at the saddle. We stood for a long time.

"Mr. Munro's coming home tomorrow. Reckon I won't be giving you a ride to school anymore with him back. Reckon it would make your grandfather happy if I didn't come around no more."

She didn't answer. I couldn't think of anything more to say. She didn't say anything, either. Finally, I reached down and straightened the stirrup and pushed my foot into it. I gave a little bounce with my down foot and started to swing onto Ginger's back.

"Don't leave, John Priddle." Kalola said without looking up at me.

Almost to the saddle, my knee kind of gave way, and I dropped back to the ground.

"What?"

She looked at me with those big, brown eyes.

"I do not want you to leave," she repeated. "Once there were many homes—many families—nearby. When I was young, I had friends and children to play with." She looked away. "Then Dole came with big money. Families left for Lahaina Town or Honolulu to make more money. Now there are pineapples where people used to live." She spun around and folded her arms.

"Now I have no friend."

Frowning, I stared at the back of her head.

"How about all the girls at school? Ruth and Ester and Tatsu and all of them?"

"I only see Ruth and Ester and Tatsu at school.

Never in summertime. The Hawaiian children live at Keomuku on the far side of island. Maybe I see them one or two times during summer."

"That's all?"

"That's all." With a shrug, she turned to look at me. "John Priddle is a good friend. Now you're going away, too."

"Least you got *some* friends," I mumbled into the saddle. "Shoot! None of the guys will even play with me. Every time I go around them, they take off like I got the pox or something. Least you got friends at school."

"You are haole," she said softly. "Everyone on the island think that all haole are like Mr. Jacobs. They feel like all haole hate them. They don't know John Priddle is a friend. My friend."

When I looked up, she was so close that our foreheads were almost touching. I could see the little pools of water that gathered at the bottom of her brown eyes.

"You're my friend, too." I said. "My best friend."

Suddenly the water that had gathered at the bottom of her eyes began to leak out. The little drops rolled down her cheek. Left glistening trails on her soft brown face. Without another word, she spun and raced to the house.

I watched her go. I wanted to stop her. I wanted to make her feel better. I wanted her tears to go away and that pretty smile to come back. My eyes turned to her grandfather. He hacked at the big leaves and the mud around them with his hoe. I felt my eyes tighten.

But it wasn't his fault. He had a right to be mad. It wasn't his fault at all—it was my fault.

I had to go tell him how sorry I was. Had to talk to him and . . . and . . .

My hands trembled. He'd probably hit me. He'd probably slug me with his fist or try to knock my head off with that hoe. It didn't matter.

I turned and started toward him. The shaking worked its way up my arms to my shoulders. I couldn't let it end like this. I couldn't just hop on Ginger and ride off with Kalola crying. I couldn't leave my friend.

I sloshed through the mud. Never slowed down. The shaking crept across my back and down my spine. I felt like I was gonna knock myself apart from the inside out. I didn't stop. Not until I was right in front of Makalii Pukui.

His old, wrinkled, angry face lifted from the work at his feet. Dark eyes cut right into me.

I wanted to turn and run. I wanted to race to Ginger, jump on her back and ride for home as fast as I could.

"Mr. Pukui . . ." I took a deep breath to keep my voice from shaking. "We need to talk!"

Chapter 18

I'm not sure what surprised me more. Whether it was the fact that he didn't hit me or that he smiled, dropped his hoe, and wrapped his arms around me.

Next thing I knew, he was calling for Kalola to come out of the house. He made us sit on the step. He stood in front of us, his hands out and his palms up.

"Makalii Pukui is an old man," he began, his voice soft and gentle. "Old man see Kalola as granddaughter. Not see that she grow to young woman. It surprise him. Mad because he not see sooner."

Kalola glanced down at her feet. I could see a little red creep into her cheeks. I pulled my eyes from her and looked back to the old man.

"John Priddle say that he sorry for look on Kalola. Say Kalola be sorry for look at John." He shook his head. "Why you two say this? Why sorry?"

Neither of us looked up. Other than a slight shrug, we didn't answer. Finally, Makalii cleared his throat.

"Okay, we start again." He managed to catch my eye, but for only an instant. "John? Why you look at Kalola?"

I didn't want to answer, but I could tell he wasn't gonna let me off the hook. I cleared my throat, just like he had done.

"Well . . . I guess . . . well . . . it was 'cause she didn't hardly have no clothes on, I reckon."

"Never see girl before?" He frowned.

"Not that much girl!" My eyes kind of crossed. "I mean . . . she didn't hardly have nothing on."

"It is my fault," Kalola said, looking at her grandfather and not at me. "I saw bathing clothes that girls and women wear in big book at Mercantile. Saw them one time when we fished near Maui, too. But this takes money." She shot a quick glance in my direction. "We do not have much money." She turned back to her grandfather.

"Two years ago Lehua, my friend who lives at Keomuku, wanted me to go with her to swim with other girls in ocean. Boys, too. She gave me short boy pants and undershirt from her older brother. Two years, this is okay. But this time, now I cannot get pants to button. Little, white shirt too tight." She gave a disgusted snort and a little shrug. "I am sorry."

Makalii coughed. "Sorry that you grow up? You look plenty funny if get old as me and still look like little girl. We have talked of growing up—of the changes that will come. You forget this?"

Kalola shook her head. "No. It's just . . . just . . . it never bothered me before. Pants would not button. Undershirt would not work. Cannot wear school clothes to swim, so I made my own swim clothes. I saw grandfather in malo, so I made one for me. Used extra cloth to cover top. It covers me a lot better than little white shirt." With a sigh, she let her shoulders sag. "Guess I was wrong."

Makalii made a little clicking sound with his tongue and shook his head. "Long, long time ago, when I was young boy, girls and women wear *pau*."

Kalola and I both frowned at him.

"Cloth that wraps around waist. And that is all they wear."

I blinked a couple of times and felt the heat rush to my face.

"Little boys and girls did not even wear clothes," Makalii went on. "There is no need for little children. But missionaries come. Everyone had to wear clothes. Now everything big secret. People always want to know big secret, so spend much time thinking about. I feel it is better to know—that way not have to spend so much time wondering." He turned back to me. "What do girls wear when swim in ocean back in Oklahoma?"

"We ain't got an ocean in Oklahoma. We swim in the farm ponds. Only, there ain't no girls along."

"So, this be first time you see girl wear clothes to swim. No clothes to hide legs or shoulders or tummy—big surprise, huh?"

"Big surprise," I agreed. "More like kind of a shock, really."

"Kalola?" He asked, turning to her.

She didn't say anything. He put a hand on her knee. "Kalola, you see many men and boys dressed in swim things, no shirt, even malo, when fish at Keomuku town. Why you look at John?"

Her mouth opened, like she was going to say something. Then she clamped her lips shut and shook her head.

Makalii cocked an eyebrow. "Maybe see John Priddle with different eyes than see other boys?"

"Maybe." Her answer was barely a whisper. "I guess he's sort of different. I like John. He's cute."

The heat rushed to my face. I thought my forehead was gonna blow the hair clean off my head. I squirmed so much, it's a wonder I didn't get splinters from the wooden step.

"Does John like Kalola? Maybe think she cute, too?"

"Yeah . . . well, sort of . . . for a girl." My voice trailed off to a whisper that was even softer than Kalola's. "I guess I like her, too. And I reckon that she's . . . well, she's sort of pretty . . . I guess."

I braced for his laughter.

Makalii didn't laugh. When he didn't, I looked at him.

"I am not mad because you two look. This is natural. Not angry for this. Angry because head and eyes must be on ocean. If not, you not see the tiger. But tiger see you. Angry because not want to lose Kalola to tiger like lose Luka."

Frowning, I turned to Kalola. I had no idea what the old man was going on about. But before I could ask, I felt him pat my knee.

"We talk of this, later. First think maybe we better have aloha talk."

I frowned. Kalola turned red again. I blinked a couple of times and leaned toward Makalii.

"I thought aloha meant 'hello' or 'good-bye.' "

He nodded. "But also mean 'I love you.' " He folded his bottom lip into his mouth and kind of nibbled on one edge of it. "One word mean many things in Hawaiian. Haole say love. Just one word. But love mean many, many things." He studied us a moment. Smiled. "John is thirteen? Fourteen?"

"Fourteen."

"Kalola is thirteen," he said.

"Almost fourteen," she insisted.

Makalii nodded. "No longer children. Bet you speak of love with friends, right?"

I heard a gulping sound when I swallowed the knot in my throat. "Back home, the older guys at school . . . we used to go out by the plum patch, just off the playground."

"Kalola?"

"While girls mend fishing nets at Keomuku," her voice was even softer than mine. "Older girls talk. I listen."

I felt my mouth drop open when I turned to stare at her. She gave a little shrug and turned back to her grandfather.

Makalii heaved a heavy sigh. "Bet they all make big secret of love. Giggle and make faces and talk in whispers."

Kalola and I nodded.

"That is the trouble with young," Makalii gave a little snort. "The young always learn of love from the young. Everyone in big rush." His smile was kind and gentle. "First, learn of love. When we know what love is, it is much easier to talk about."

Chapter 19

How long we sat and visited with the gentle old man, I have no idea. Kalola and I didn't look at each other. We just visited—not only hearing Makalii's words, but feeling them as he spoke.

I didn't even realize Kalola and I had been leaning against one another. Our shoulders supporting one another and the sides of our heads were touching as we talked and listened. The first time I even noticed was when Makalii put his hands on the ground and started to get up. Only he didn't. He kind of struggled a moment, then held his hands out to us.

We both leaped up to help him.

"Old knees not work so good no more." He glanced to the ocean. "Time to go home now, John Priddle. Your mama and papa worry about you, like I worry about Kalola if not home by *ahiahi*. But hope you come back soon."

He shuffled up the steps. Kalola and I went to get Ginger.

"*Ahiahi* means 'evening,' " Kalola explained before I could even ask. I put the reins over Ginger's saddle horn and held them with one hand.

"What was that tiger stuff he was talking about earlier? It didn't make any sense. Look, even though I'm from Oklahoma, I *know* there ain't no tigers swimming around out there in the ocean. And who is Luka?"

Kalola wrapped her arms about herself and turned from me.

"Luka was my mother. Tiger is a shark. Tiger shark took Mother and Father from me."

I could see her sides jerk in and out beneath the white blouse. Figuring she was crying, I left the reins and moved around Ginger to try and comfort her. She turned her back again. I stood, not knowing what to do.

"Luka was the daughter of Makalii. She married Kioni, my father. Kioni is the same name as you—John. They were very young, but very happy. Only Luka liked haole things. Like pretty dresses and gramophone and pretty things. When Dole came, she wanted Makalii to sell land. But, Makalii would not leave home."

I reached out a hand to touch her shoulder. Then, I drew it back.

"So . . . what happened?"

"Luka and Kioni went to Niihau. In shallows near island, there are many oysters with · many pearls. Haole think black pearl is the prettiest and most rare. They pay big money. My parents make many trips, find lots of pearls, and get rich. But Luka was not happy to be a little rich. She wanted to be big rich. Last time they go to Niihau to look for black pearls, others who went with them saw the tigers come. But Luka had eyes only for pearls. Not on ocean."

"And that's why your grandfather got so mad. He didn't want you watching me when you was supposed to be watching for sharks and stuff?"

Kalola sniffed and nodded.

"Tiger took my mother. Kioni tried to save her. Tigers take Kioni, too."

Her voice broke off in a trail of sobs and tears. Not knowing what else to do, I put my arm around her and patted her shoulder. "I'm sorry" was the only thing I could think to say.

The ride back up the hill to Lanai City was probably one of the longest rides I ever took in my life.

When I was little, I always knew that things would straighten out when I got older. I'd know stuff. The world and the people in it wouldn't be so confusing and hard to understand, once I got bigger. Because when you're big, you know all there is to know.

Seemed like I was more confused now than ever. "Kalola's grandfather likes me. I like him. Kalola's my best friend and wants to stay my friend. Only, now that she's a girl, being friends is a lot different.

"Well, I mean . . . she was a girl all along . . . but, I guess I just never noticed before. But why can't girls and boys be friends? I guess we can, only we can't go fishing and stuff together. But we like doing things together and being around one another and talking. So, why can't we do stuff like going fishing?"

* * *

I didn't even realize I was talking to myself until Ginger stopped. I blinked a couple of times and looked around. She stood at the gate to the corral and turned her head to look at me. I guess she was wondering why I hadn't gotten off.

I put her tack up and headed for the house. It was almost dark when I got home.

"Wonder if Daddy ever gets confused."

"Nope."

Darned if I wasn't talking to myself again. I didn't even realize it—much less expect somebody to answer.

Daddy was sitting on the porch. A magazine was folded in his lap, and he smiled up at me.

"Huh?" I said when I spotted him.

"You asked if Daddy ever got confused," he repeated. "And I said nope."

"How come?" I frowned.

"I stay that way. You can't *get* what you already got. I started getting confused a long time ago and just decided it was easier to stay that way."

I sort of shook my head. I guess he was trying to be funny. It wasn't a very good joke.

"I'm serious. What do you do about it?"

"About being confused?"

"Yes, sir."

He shrugged and got to his feet. "I don't know. What are you confused about?"

I shrugged back. "Just stuff."

"What kind of stuff?"

I wanted to tell him. I wanted to ask his advice and his help—only, I couldn't.

"Just stuff," I repeated.

He shot me a disgusted look.

"A whole bunch of stuff," I tried to explain without really telling him anything. "All sorts of things, all mixed up inside my head. And I can't sort 'em out. You ever get that way?"

"Yeah."

"So what do you do about it?"

Daddy seemed to study me for a long time. Finally, he sighed and reached to open the front door.

"Your mama's waiting supper."

"What do you do?"

"I guess, what I try to do is pick the one thing that's bothering me the most. Try to figure out how to solve that one thing. Once that's out of the way, I move on to the next."

My eyes flashed. I felt the smile tug at my cheeks.

Chapter 20

Kalola slugged me on the arm as hard as she could. *Some friend,* I thought. I rubbed the sore spot.

"Hey! What did you do that for?"

She glared at me.

"For not telling me what your idea is. You made me wait all day in school. I couldn't think about lessons. Dirty trick! You should have told me this morning instead of making me wait."

She doubled her fist again. I held my hands up and waved them back and forth.

"Now wait. Just hold on," I sputtered. "Okay, what it boils down to is that summer's here. Only one more week of school. Come summer, you're gonna spend a bunch of time fishing with your grandfather. Only, I can't go with you 'cause I keep looking at you. You're a girl. And you keep looking at me. I'm a boy, right? So what's the one thing we have to do?"

She raised her fist.

"You tell me."

"I can't tell you. I got to show you. Come on."

* * *

Ted Jacobs was throwing his baseball on the roof of his house. Over and over and over again, he'd throw it and wait for it to roll down. Most times he caught it; sometimes he missed. It took an eternity for the baseball to finally go too high on the roof. The second it rolled over the peak of the house, I felt my muscles tense.

I grabbed Kalola's hand. We were crouched like runners fixing to start a race, and as soon as Ted walked around the house, I gave her hand a yank. We sprinted across Mr. Munro's backyard, across our backyard, and leaped to the porch. I shoved Kalola inside, jumped in behind her and slammed the door, just as Ted came back around his house.

We stood there a moment, panting and catching our breath. Then I tugged on her hand. She stopped.

"This is your home?"

With a sneer I glanced back at her.

"No, I'm just breaking into some stranger's house."

I tugged her hand again. She frowned.

"I'm teasing," I said. "Yes. It's my home."

She followed me toward my room, only she kept stopping and asking what all the stuff was. At the rate we were going, we'd never get through the house 'cause I had to stop and answer:

"It's a washing machine."

"A cook stove."

"An icebox."

"What?"

"An icebox," I repeated. "Twice a week, when the

pineapple barge comes back from Honolulu, this guy brings a big block of ice on his truck and . . ."

"What is ice?" she interrupted.

I sighed. My shoulders slumped when I turned to glare at her.

"Look, if there's time when we get done, I'll *show* you. Now come on!"

Sunday night, I had already sorted stuff and had it hidden in the corner of my closet. Kalola sat on the edge of the bed while I dug it out.

"Here," I said, stuffing her things into her hands. "Put this on. I'll go in Mama's and Daddy's room and get mine on. Soon as we're dressed, we'll yell at each other and meet in the hall to see how it looks."

She frowned at the pile of clothes in her hands. "Why?"

"Just do it!" I ordered. I grabbed my stuff, closed the door behind me, and scurried down the hall.

Kalola yelled before I quite had my jeans buttoned. I guess the old, discarded Levi's were a little tighter than the last time I wore them. I sucked in my stomach and squeezed the last two buttons into the button holes.

When we met in the hall, I couldn't keep the smile off my face. With my baggy, old jeans on and my work shirt with the undershirt beneath it—shoot, I couldn't even tell Kalola was a girl.

We stood in front of my mirror. I smiled. Kalola just looked disgusted.

"What?" I asked, finally.

She didn't answer. She only stood there, staring at

our reflections in the mirror with that irritated expression on her face.

"What?" I repeated.

Kalola pulled the shirttail out of her Levi's and unbuttoned the blue work shirt. Then she pulled it off and handed it to me. The old undershirt I had handed Kalola wasn't nearly as tight on her as the old undershirt I had on was tight on me. Still . . .

"Put it back on."

"Why?"

"Your undershirt . . . it . . . you're . . . you're . . . you're a girl."

She shrugged. "You are a boy."

I frowned at my reflection. Finally, I held my hands out with the palms up. Why on earth . . .

"I'm a boy," I said, almost to myself.

She nodded. "I can still see boy under these clothes."

"I don't get it," I said helplessly.

Kalola had the blue work shirt on. She buttoned the last two buttons, tucked the tail in and pointed at the mirror. The blue work shirt was loose and floppy. My pants hung loose on her, too, and they were so long that they went clean past the end of her bare feet.

"I have got so many clothes on, you can't see a girl. But you still look like boy. I probably will look. This is not working if one doesn't look and other does look. We both gotta not look, okay?"

I shrugged. "Okay."

Chapter 21

Makalii Pukui laughed at us. He laughed so hard, I thought he was gonna shake himself apart. Finally, he sat down in the sand and buried his face in his hands.

I guess we did look kind of ridiculous. Kalola had on my blue work shirt, with an undershirt underneath, and Levi's. The pants were so loose on her, she had to hang onto a belt loop to keep them from falling off. The legs were so long, they ended a good five inches past the tips of her toes. I probably looked about the same in Daddy's old work shirt and his baggy Levi's. Fact was, I had to hold onto a belt loop to keep from losing them.

It was really disappointing. We spent Monday afternoon, finding the right clothes and managed to get out of the house without Ted Jacobs or anyone seeing us. We talked about stuff on the rides to and from school on Tuesday, then brought our swimming outfits for Makalii Pukui to approve of.

We stood there, glaring at him. Finally, when he

seemed to catch his breath and lifted his face from his hands, Kalola pointed to me with her free hand.

"You didn't want us to look, so we would keep our eyes out for tiger," she announced. "Dressed like this, we won't look."

The old man took a deep breath and struggled to his feet.

"You no look, okay," he snorted. "So many clothes get wet, you go straight to bottom of ocean."

He stepped between us. "Got to not look, but also got to swim. Wait here."

In a moment, he came back from the house. In his hand, he carried a knife and a long piece of rope. He took the rope and cut it in half, handing a piece to each of us.

"First thing is keep pants up."

We laced our strands of rope through our belt loops and tied them with a knot. With our hands free, we both put our fists on our hips and turned to glare at him.

"Feet need to kick water. Got to have free so can swim." When he had the bottoms of our Levi's cut off, he stepped back. "Both okay with this?"

We nodded.

Makalii smiled. "Okay. Both got feet. Both got ankles. Pull pants up to knees." When we did as we were told, he asked, "Still okay?"

"Okay." We nodded.

He had us let go of our pants. He came back and cut them off just above the knees.

"Now pull up higher."

He cut the bottoms of our Levi's off again, just below the pockets. Then he cut the sleeves off our shirts.

We both stood there with our cut off Levi's and sleeveless shirts.

"This look like best we can do," he sighed. "Still a lot of clothes. But we give it a try."

It worked.

I mean, it really worked! Not only did Kalola and I not look at each other, but I also found there was a whole different world under the ocean.

We swam at the east side of Hulopoe Bay. It was a good walk down the beach from the shack, but well worth it. There was a reef there and a high cliff on one side. Makalii sat above us on the rocks. Kalola told me if he blew the conch shell, we must get from the water *wikki wikki*—that meant 'really fast.' He watched and we swam.

There was a world beneath the waves that I'd never seen before. A world I'd never imagined. A wondrous, fascinating world.

There were fish of every shape and size. Through the bamboo goggles, the colors were bright and crisp and clear as any rainbow in the sky. Yellow fish, blue fish, black ones with little splotches of red near their heads and yellow fans on their tails. Just as Kalola had warned me, the coral was sharp. I didn't mean to, but

I latched onto it one time and came back up with a little cut on my palm and things that looked like little black stickers in my fingers. I had to dig them out with my teeth. It hurt like the devil.

Another thing I had to learn—a thing that was real hard—was not to stay down too long. I'd suck in a deep breath of air, then get interested in all the things there were to see. All of a sudden, I'd realize I needed to breathe. Only, when I'd look up . . . I was way the heck down there! A couple of times, I just barely made it to the surface before my lungs burst.

Kalola swam with me. I'd point at stuff, and when we got back to the surface, she'd tell me what it was. Lots of things . . . well . . . she didn't even know the names of, herself. Others . . .

"Cup coral," she answered.

"They look like little, yellow buttercups, only with feathers on the end."

"Not flowers. Coral. Tiny animals who live together and make the reef."

"How about that bright purple thing with the yellow around the edges."

"Flatworm. There are many on the reef. All different colors."

She was right. Some flatworms were all one color. One looked like a tiger—mostly yellow with black, tiger stripes on it. Another reminded me of a leopard. It was mostly black but had yellow spots.

The next time we surfaced:

"Awela." She answered when I pointed at the fish with bold stripes of pink and blue.

"The yellow one? Solid yellow from stem to stern. He's kinda cute."

"Laipala."

"The one what looks like a squirrel with them big, black eyes?"

"Uu."

One time, Kalola tapped me on the arm and pointed. I didn't see it at first, but she kept pointing. There was the weirdest looking fish I'd ever seen in my life. It was kind of an orangish brown with a few white stripes. It blended in perfectly with the rocks where it rested on the bottom. The thing had these long spines or fins sticking out all around. Like I said—weird. When we got back to the surface for air, Kalola told me it was a lionfish. She warned me to be careful and never grab one or step on it. The spines were sharp and very poisonous.

"Tomorrow last day of school?" Makalii Pukui asked, when we finally came back to the beach.

With smiles that stretched clear across our faces, Kalola and I both nodded.

Makalii smiled back.

"Tomorrow, we go to *pukas* and find bait. Kioni Priddle, you spend night so we get early start next morning. Go catch fish."

I was so excited, I wanted to tell the old man every single thing I had seen. I wanted to ask him the names of stuff Kalola didn't know.. I wanted to tell him how wonderful and exciting it was under the ocean.

But, when he said, "... spend the night...," all the excitement just sort of whooshed out of me. How in the world could I ever talk Mama and Daddy into letting me spend the night?

Chapter 22

Timing is probably the most important thing. When a fella needs to ask his parents something that he's pretty sure the answer to is gonna be "no"—well, timing is critical.

The Jacobses helped.

Fact is, that night at supper was probably the first time I really liked the Jacobses, ever since I got here. That's 'cause Mama and Daddy were busy fussing about them and not hardly paying me much attention at all.

Daddy was upset with Paul Jacobs on account of the chaps. He first thought that Mr. Jacobs hadn't been able to get hold of George Munro before he returned from the big island to Lanai. Then he found out that Paul Jacobs didn't even bother to call him or Captain Sanches. When Daddy told him again how well the leather chaps protected his legs from the pineapple and how the workers needed them, Paul Jacobs just laughed it off and told him to forget it.

"Calls them kanakas," Daddy said. "It means 'commoner' or 'worker'. Only the way Paul says it, he makes it sound like 'dirt'."

Mama wasn't too tickled with Mrs. Jacobs, either. Seems she was sweeter than maple syrup to Mama or Mrs. du Chance—the French chemist's wife—or to Mr. Foster. But when any of the Filipino or Japanese women came in, Mrs. Jacobs was real snooty or sharp with them.

"This Hawaiian woman came in the other day," Mama began. "Walked clean from the other side of the island with about five dozen eggs to sell." She stopped, kind of shaking a finger at Daddy. "Now we only had about a half dozen eggs left in the whole store, but Carmine up and tells her, real snooty-like, that we don't need any eggs and . . ."

They were right wrapped up with their conversation about the Jacobses. Now was the time to jump in.

"Can I spend the night with my friend tomorrow?"

". . . and finally Carmine said she'd take them," Mama kept right on talking like she hadn't even heard me. "But she only paid her half a cent each. Shoot, we pay a penny and a half for eggs from Oahu. And she only offered the woman half a cent. What really bothered me was the way . . ."

"Can I spend the night with my friend tomorrow?" I asked again. "We're gonna get up early and go fishing."

"Don't interrupt while someone's talking, John," Daddy said. "What were you saying, Helen?"

"I said that what really bothered me was the way she treated the poor woman," Mama went on.

Daddy nodded his agreement. "It's the same with Paul. He's always been polite and nice to me or Mr. du Chance, but when it comes to the workers . . ."

He sighed. Both shook their heads and looked really exasperated.

"Can I go fishing with my friend?"

Daddy glanced at me and cocked an eyebrow.

"We need to get a real early start on Saturday, so I need to spend the night. Okay?"

He frowned. "Just the two of you?"

"No." I shook my head. "My friend's grandfather is taking us. He's really a good fisherman. He really knows what he's doing."

Daddy glanced at Mama. She was still thinking about Mrs. Jacobs. She kind of stared off into space, and I could tell she wasn't listening to either of us.

"You know," Mama said more to the ceiling than to Daddy. "She's got a whole other set of books in the back room. I saw her working on them one day. Wonder why she'd have two sets of books? Nobody has a second set of books—not unless they're trying to hide something. But what? I'm tempted to sneak in one of these days and . . ."

"Can I, Dad?" I whispered.

He gave a quick nod in my direction, then went back to the conversation.

"Helen, you shouldn't pry into other folks' business."

Mama shrugged. "Well, I really wouldn't sneak in and prowl around in her desk. Still, why would someone need two sets of books, unless they were doing something wrong?"

Mama and Daddy kept talking about the Jacobses. It wasn't like them. Daddy hardly ever talked bad about nobody. But I guess the Jacobses just brought out the worst in both of them.

Daddy said that Paul Jacobs never did a lick of work. Mama said that's 'cause he was the foreman. But Daddy said as how he'd been with a number of foreman or bosses who worked every bit as hard as their men did. He said all Paul Jacobs did was go around pouring dye into the little pools where water disappeared into the rocks, then trying to spot where it came out. "Don't make any sense. Especially on this side of the island. I mean, wherever it comes out, it's still gonna be in the pineapples. So why bother? What's he hunting for? What's he up to?"

I eased up from the couch and slipped off to my bedroom. I went to sleep with a big smile on my face that night, proud of myself for how well my timing had worked.

The boat was weird. It wasn't like the boat Charlie and I fished from on Whitener's Pond. Made from a single log, Makalii Pukui's boat was long and slim and pointed on both ends. The inside was hollowed out and I could see burned or singed marks all up and down the sides. Two poles arched out from the right side, connecting to another pointed, boatlike thing there. Only the one on the side wasn't hollowed out.

Kalola said it was what we haole called an outrigger. The thing at the side helped balance the boat and made it more stable in rough water or when people were jumping around, trying to land a big fish.

As big as the boat was, it was surprisingly light. In the very center of the boat was a raised spot with a hole hollowed out in the middle of it. Makalii brought a long pole with cloth wrapped around it. I guess it was a sail and the raised spot with the hole was where he put it in.

We tugged and pulled and pushed and grunted until the boat was finally in the water. About waist deep or so, Kalola and I jumped in, grabbed our paddles and started digging the water. Makalii pushed a few more steps, then he jumped in.

The paddles were a little different from the oars on the Whitener's boat. Instead of fitting onto swivels on the sides, we held these in our hands. And instead of being flat on the bottom, these paddles were like a sharp, pointed leaf on the end of a stick. They worked fine, though, and in a moment or two we were well on our way.

That's when it hit me. The up and down and sway and swell of the ocean. I felt my eyes flash. I spun to face Kalola and her grandfather.

"I'm gonna get seasick. I can feel it, already. I'm gonna . . ."

"Shut mouth," Makalii roared from the back of the boat. "Shut mouth and paddle. We get past breakers, I will fix."

About fifty yards from the beach, there was a smooth area. Toward the shore, waves swelled, turned white, and broke on the sandy shore. Toward the ocean, more waves rolled in, only to break and foam white against something beneath the water that I couldn't see. But where Makalii let us stop paddling—well, it was smooth and almost calm.

"See the line where the ocean meet the sky?" Makalii called from behind me.

I nodded.

"Kioni Priddle keep eyes on that line. Keep eyes where ocean meet sky."

I did as he told me. In a moment, Kalola tapped me on the shoulder. When I turned, she handed me something. I glanced down at what looked like wet wood shavings.

"Put in corner of mouth," Makalii said. He stuck his finger in his mouth between his back teeth and his cheek. "Put there, but do not bite. Can move around in mouth." With his finger still inside his mouth, he drug it between his teeth and gums to show me. "Eyes on line where ocean meet sky and gingerroot in mouth—no seasick."

At first the stuff tasted really sweet. But it took only a second or two before a spicy, HOT feel hit. I had to move it, real quick, to keep from burning a hole in my cheek. Don't rightly know what it was. Either the gingerroot really kept my stomach from feeling the roll of the ocean, or I was so busy moving it around in my mouth—to keep it from burning—that I didn't have time to think about being seasick.

Whatever—it worked.

Kalola and I spent the rest of the afternoon, diving into the pukas to catch lobsters, and not once did I feel the slightest bit seasick.

Chapter 23

Pukas were great holes in the shallow reef. The smooth water between the ocean and the shore was where the reef ran. In places it wasn't more than four or five feet deep. Then, all of a sudden, this dark hole would open up beneath our outrigger.

Makalii would keep the boat there while Kalola and I dived in. Some of the pukas were only ten to fifteen feet wide and not very deep. Others would be maybe forty feet across and the center of them so bottomless, I couldn't even make it down.

We searched the edges and bottoms of the pukas for lobsters. When Kalola brought the first one up, it didn't take long to figure what we were looking for. Lobsters were like giant crawdads. I mean, just exactly like crawdads, only bigger. The ones Kalola called Hawaiian lobsters were easy to find. They were a bright red in color and easy to spot in the dark blue water. The Slipper lobsters were different. I guess they called them Slipper lobsters, 'cause if I used my wildest imagination, the things did kind of resemble a woman's slipper. Still, they blended into the rock and coral, almost as well as the lionfish did. For the life of me, I couldn't figure out how Kalola managed to find them.

By evening the bottom of our outrigger was virtually crawling with crawdads—I mean lobsters. They were climbing all over one another and snapping and fighting and stuff. Instead of watching the line where the ocean met the sea, I kept glancing down at the bottom of the boat. I just knew one of the creepy things was gonna latch onto my toe or something. Makalii slid the boat up on the shore, slick as a whistle. Once we'd pulled the outrigger onto the bank, Kalola took three of the bigger lobsters and went to the house. First thing I did was spit the gingerroot out and rinse my mouth with water from the gourd in the bottom of the boat. Then the old man and I snapped the lobsters that were left in half.

We dropped the tails in a tin bucket. In another bucket, we dropped the rest of the lobsters. The old man got a big stick and used it to smash up the heads, bodies, and claws. He kept picking up handfuls of sand and mixing it with the crushed up mess.

When we finished, we washed our hands in the ocean with sand and went to the house. I put on my clean underwear, Levi's, and a dry work shirt. Then went to find where my friend was.

Kalola stood between the shack and a big, black pot. She wore a dresslike thing. Made of bright cloth, it wrapped around and was tied with a knot on her right shoulder.

The pot beside her was held above a roaring fire by

a couple of wooden poles and a crossbar. I could see steam rising from the boiling water. Makalii came from the shack with three wooden plates. Kalola got a couple of sticks and used them to lift a lobster out of the pot for each of us. We sat cross-legged with the plates in our laps.

There was no way I was gonna eat a lobster. I mean the things were still whole—the eyes, sticking up on those little pole things, were still staring at me.

Despite my protests, Kalola and her grandfather finally talked me into giving it a try. They showed me how to break the claws and dig the white meat out with a sharp stick. Then they showed me how to snap the tail open and peel it back so I could get at that meat.

I've got to admit, no matter how ugly those lobsters looked, the claws and tails were some of the sweetest, best meat I ever ate in my life.

We sat and visited by the fire until it was nothing but soft, red coals. Finally, Makalii groaned and got to his feet. I could hear his old knees pop when he stood.

"Sleep now. Get up early to catch Ulua." He turned to us. "Kalola have mat for Kioni to sleep."

She nodded. "In big room," then to me, "but you can move to the porch if you want to sleep outside."

Makalii smiled and shuffled off toward the shack.

Trouble was, neither one of us were sleepy. We talked for a while, then walked down to the beach. There we walked and talked some more.

We were about halfway to the big rock cliffs at the east end of Hulopoe Bay when I noticed that we were holding hands. It kinda shocked me at first. I mean, I hadn't even noticed. Only instead of trying to get loose, like I did back home when Amanda Burke got hold of me, I just kept walking.

Having Kalola's hand in mine felt natural as could be. It felt like her hand belonged there.

Before the sun came up, Makalii Pukui quietly shuffled into the living room and nudged me with his foot. I guess Kalola and I had spent more time walking and talking on the beach than I figured. It was sure hard to get my eyes open and follow Makalii outside. I had kind of a throbbing headache, too.

We went to the far end of his taro patch and dug around in the dirt beside this little tree. It was still so dark, I was barely able to see the chunk of root he pulled up and handed to me. It smelled sweet, though. Next, I followed him to a little spring. Water seeped from the rocks to fill a pool that was about as big around as our bathtub at home. Then it trickled over the edge of the pool to keep the taro field soggy and damp.

"You need to know how to do this," he announced, handing me the knife. "I not gather gingerroot for you each time we go fish. You need know how. I show this time."

He took the root and sloshed it back and forth in the water to get the dirt off. Taking my hand, he showed me how to whittle some of the bark off until I had a handful of shavings. Again, we dipped that into the water and sloshed it around until it was clean.

"Put in pocket," he instructed. "Take out and put in mouth if need to."

"This pocket? Don't we need our swimming stuff?"

He shook his head.

"Today we fish from boat. Not go in ocean."

We got Kalola up, loaded stuff in the outrigger, and paddled from the shore before first light.

Makaiwa Point was protected from the waves by Lanai itself. It was at the very edge of the island, so we could see Maui and the sunrise. Makalii put the lobster tails from one bucket onto big hooks attached to the end of ropes. Once the hooks were baited and thrown into the water, he began tossing handfuls of the ground-up lobster and sand from the other bucket. It floated for a moment, then sank to be swept out to sea on the currents beneath our boat.

"How long we got to sit here?" I asked, feeling the rise and fall of the boat.

"Not long," he answered. "Honu already come. Ulua not far behind."

"*Honu* is 'sea turtle,'" Kalola whispered from behind me.

Makalii pointed. I followed the aim of his finger. Not far from the boat, three little heads bobbed up and down in the waves. But when I looked closer, they weren't so little. They were turtle heads, all right.

Only the things were big around as both my fists put together. They worked their way might near to the boat. In the water, they looked as big around as I was. Suddenly they spotted us, flipped around, and swam off like a shot.

I held the rope, moved the gingerroot to my other cheek with my tongue, and waited.

Suddenly the rope jerked. It wasn't like a little tug at the end of a fishing line back home. This thing jerked! It jerked hard. Then the rope took off in my hands.

I tried to hang on, but the rope whizzed through my grip so fast it felt like my palms and fingers were on fire. I ground my teeth together. Squeezed hard as I could. The rope stopped its burning rush through my hands. My eyes flashed wide when the outrigger snapped around. We sped off, the bow of the boat slipping through the waves on its wild rush to chase the rope.

Chapter 24

"My lord, John!"

That's about all Mama could say when I yelled at her and she came out of the house and saw the fish tied to Ginger's saddle horn.

Daddy followed her. "What in the world is that?" he gasped. "That thing's huge!"

I smiled proudly and swung down from the saddle.

"It's an ahi. A tuna. The Hawaiians call it a 'fire fish.' That's 'cause your hands get so hot trying to pull 'em in; the rope feels like it's on fire."

I held my hands out toward them. Mama let out a little gasp when she saw the busted blisters and blood on my hands. Daddy just shook his head.

"We thought it was an ulua," I said. "That's what we were fishing for, anyhow. But when I tried to wrap the rope around my hand to help hold it, Makalii jumped clean over Kalola and thumped me upside the head. He could tell it was an ahi—even while the thing was still way under the water. He said if I wrapped the rope around my hand, it would end up yanking me in the water and I'd be feeding the fish instead of catchin' it to feed myself."

I untied the rope. Ginger shied to the side when I took the fish loose. She hadn't much cared about carrying the big, floppy thing up the hill in the first place. When I had it off, I laid it on the porch, folded my arms and smiled up at Mama and Daddy.

"Ain't bad for my first time fishing, is it?" I boasted.

"How many of these did you get?" Daddy frowned.

The smile tugged clean up to my ears.

"Just this one. But it took me the biggest part of the day to land him. Did it all by myself. We're going again tomorrow. Can I? And if we catch more than one, we're gonna go around the island to Keomuku. Makalii says that ahi run in schools—whole bunches of them together. We're gonna try to catch us some more. If we do, we're gonna go over to Keomuku and share what we catch. Fishermen always share their catch. Anyway, Hawaiian fishermen—that's what they do. Can I go? Huh, can I? Please?"

I got a knife from the kitchen and cut off fillets of the tuna. Makalii already had it gutted. He had taken a big chunk off one side for him and Kalola. I cut the meat off the bones, only instead of looking neat and clean, like the old man had left it, well . . . my filleting was kind of messy. I didn't get the meat off very well and left good, big chunks of meat hanging on the bone. But with a little practice . . .

Mama baked part of it in the oven. The rest she put in the icebox, down next to the ice so it would save.

We ate until we were might near ready to bust. Afterwards Daddy and I helped with the dishes, then Mama and Daddy settled down in front of the radio, and I went out on the porch.

It wasn't long before Daddy came out to join me.

"You and Mama decide if I could go fishing tomorrow?" I asked.

Daddy didn't answer. He made a grunting sound when he sat down on the porch beside me and patted his full tummy.

"We're still thinking on it, John. Only . . . I think there's something you and I need to talk about, first."

Something about the tone of his voice sent a little chill racing up my back. I leaned against the post beside me and turned to face him.

"Okay," I said—more like asked.

He cleared his throat. Then he sat for a long time, staring out at the pineapple fields before he cleared his throat again.

"José de los Santos and me have become pretty good friends," he began. "We work together and all that stuff. He's been here on Lanai for three years. Knows a lot of people." He lowered his head and looked up at me. "José knows some of the Hawaiians, too."

I didn't say anything when he paused. All of a sudden, I wished I hadn't eaten so much baked fish. That's 'cause the knot that yanked in my stomach made me feel like I was gonna throw up.

"José tells me there's only one Hawaiian family on this side of the island."

Now the knot was working its way up into my chest.

"He tells me all the Hawaiians except Makalii Pukui live over by Keomuku—on the far side of the island."

Now the lump was in my throat.

"He tells me that no other Hawaiians but Makalii and his granddaughter, Carol, live on this side of the island. You know something else?"

I made a gulping sound when I tried to force the knot back down. I shook my head.

"You know what the Hawaiian name for Carol is?"

Reluctantly, I nodded and looked him square in the eye.

"What is it?"

"Kalola." I swallowed again.

"That's your friend's name—Kalola, right?"

I looked at the ground and nodded.

Daddy sat for a long, long time. Neither of us spoke or looked at one another. Finally, Mama came out. She stood beside him for a while, then sat down. At last, Daddy took a deep breath.

"Your mama's been wanting me to talk to you about boys and girls for a long time. I guess I forgot. Or, maybe ... well ... maybe I just been putting it off. Reckon it's about time we had us this talk. All three of us."

"I already know about boys and girls," I told them, without taking my eyes from the ground.

"What do you know?" Daddy asked.

"Well, first off ... there's a lot more to love than what the big guys talk about at school."

"At school?" Daddy asked. "You mean back in Oklahoma?"

"Yes, sir."

"Out behind the plum patch?"

I blinked and looked at Daddy.

"What plum patch?" Mama asked.

I guess my mouth kind of flopped open. I couldn't believe my daddy knew about the plum patch.

"What plum patch?" Mama repeated.

He looked at her, looked at me, then looked back at Mama.

"At the far end of the Pioneer school playground." Then, as if answering the look on my face, he shrugged. "Okay . . . it's an old plum patch. It was there when I was going to school." He turned back to Mama. "Guys talk about stuff. . . . Okay?"

I nudged him with my elbow. "Girls do, too," I confided. "Only, us guys ain't supposed to know about it."

Mama scowled at Daddy for a time. He gave a little shrug. Then both of them looked at me with arched eyebrows.

"Well . . . anyway . . . okay," I stammered. "Everybody talks about that stuff. You know, whispering and giggling and all that. Only, they hardly ever talk about love. Mr. Pukui says that young folks always go about it the wrong way—says if people knew about love *first,* then there wouldn't be any need for whispering and giggling or feeling guilty—says they wouldn't be so mixed up."

"So you're getting your information from Mr. Pukui, right?" Daddy frowned.

I shrugged. "Well, like I said, I heard some stuff from the big guys at school. But the important things—I mean, the *real* important things—that's what Mr. Pukui told us about."

"Us?" Mama's eyes were as big around as melons. Her eyebrows almost touched her bangs. "You and . . . ?"

"Me and Kalola—Carol."

"You talked about the birds'n' bees . . . you and . . . with a . . . you talked about *that* with a girl?"

I looked her square in the eye. "No, Mama. What we talked about was love. Because without love, all that other stuff ain't nothing but empty."

Chapter 25

Reckon there was a time when talking to my own mama and daddy about the things we spoke of . . . well . . . it would have been the most embarrassing thing in the world. There was a time, back in Oklahoma, when I probably would have died at even the thought of such a thing.

But that was before Makalii Pukui.

As I remembered his gentleness, his words—I wasn't embarrassed at all. I told Mama and Daddy most everything, from not having any friends at school to how Mr. Munro tricked me into giving Kalola a ride. I told them how Kalola and I became best friends and how I didn't tell them 'cause I didn't want them making fun of me and talking about a girlfriend. I went from that clean on to what Makalii Pukui had told us about aloha.

How long we talked, I'm not sure. It was way into the night. Fact was, I didn't feel like I got hardly any sleep at all when Mama and Daddy got me up the next morning.

Daddy walked over to the Jacobses and told them that he and Mama had something important to do and wouldn't be at work today. As soon as he got back, we took off down the hill.

Mama rode Ginger. Daddy and I walked.

"There's four kinds of love, right?"

I nodded. "Reckon there's more. But four main kinds."

"There's the love of knowledge." Daddy clamped three fingers down with his thumb and stuck out his index finger. "That's like black words on a white page."

"Dr. Smyth," Mama called, leaning down from Ginger's back. "Remember the math professor I had at Oklahoma College for Women? She would rather do a math problem than eat. Don't even think she had a family." She nodded her head, then kind of frowned. "And the second kind of love is for money or possessions."

Daddy looked over his shoulder at her and stuck up another finger. "Met lots more than one man in my life who loved things. Six Carolton, over to El Reno—that man spent his whole life trying to buy up land. Wanted to own the whole state. And Wes Humphry, at the Model-T dealership. Man's so tight with a dollar, he squeaks."

"Not just men." Mama shook a finger back and forth. "Bessie McArden's got so much gold jewelry collected in her house, she could start a bank."

Daddy held up a third finger. "Then there's the love a man and woman have. And . . ." Daddy kind of skipped over the third kind real quick, kept his thumb against his palm and held four fingers out at his side. ". . . the fourth is the love parents have for their child."

"That's the important one," I told him. "Makalii says it's the only *real* love there is. But it ain't just the love parents have for their kid. It's that *kind* of love."

"You said it's a real unselfish kind of love?"

"Yes, sir. That's what Makalii Pukui said. It's the kind of love you just give. Just 'cause it's somebody you care about. You love 'em and you don't expect nothing back."

"I'm really looking forward to meeting this friend of yours." Daddy's pace seemed to quicken.

Before we got to the Pukuis', I coached Mama and Daddy on poi—just like Kalola had coached me. I told them that before they got down to whatever serious talking they were going to do, we'd have to eat. "You don't talk about serious stuff around the poi bowl. Keep it light and friendly. Use your fingers. Just dip 'em in and scoop up the stuff and . . ." I told them all I could remember.

We spent the whole day with Makalii and Kalola. We all talked. We all ate poi and fish. (Mama and Daddy didn't care much for the poi, but I told them that they'd get used to it.) Then Makalii and Mama and Daddy talked alone for a long, long time. Kalola and I sat on the front steps. When they were done all three of them came to the front of the house.

Kalola and I squirmed.

Makalii sat between us.

"Kioni, your makua tell me that you say the best love is as the love a mother or father have for their child."

I nodded.

"Say you tell that when a young man and young woman share this kind of love, the love that wants only good for the other and expects nothing in return, that they know love and are ready for love."

I shrugged and gave another little nod.

Makalii's gentle smile and the way he shook his head made my shoulders sag.

"Is more."

"More?"

He nodded. "This kind of love must be inside." A gnarled, wrinkled hand reached out and touched my chest. "Must be in heart and spirit. Must not be for just one another, but for all people."

I felt my face scrunch.

"All people?"

He nodded.

"You mean even folks what are mean to you and stuff like that? Even people you don't like."

Makalii patted my chest again and nodded.

"Even more for people you not like than for people you do like."

A vision of Harvey Bouman flashed through my head. My lip curled up on one side.

"Ain't no way I could love Harvey Bouman," I blurted. My eyes rolled inside my head. "He was all the time beating up on kids. That's too hard."

Makalii sat up real straight. His head whipped around at Daddy.

"You tell boy that life be easy?"

Daddy looked me straight in the eye and shook his head. Makalii turned on Mama. "You tell boy this?" Mama smiled at me and shook her head.

"Who tell Kioni life be easy?"

My mouth kind of flopped open. "Well . . . I . . . well, nobody . . . I don't guess."

Daddy, Mama, and Mr. Pukui left me and Kalola sitting on the step with our mouths open, while they strolled down the beach again. And, again, it was an eternity before they came back with their decision.

Chapter 26

That summer on Lanai was the most fabulous summer of my life!

We fished. When the sea was choppy or when Makalii said it was not the time for fishing, Kalola and I explored. One time she took me to this place she called Kaunolu Bay. There was a cave there with strange pictures and symbols on the wall. Not far from it were the old ruins of a village. She said King Kamehameha once had a summer home at Kaunolu Village, but the ruins were all that was left.

We explored Hookio Gulch. We played hide-and-seek in the thick cover of the gorge and gathered flowers so Kalola could make a lei for Makalii's birthday. Kalola came to my house for supper a couple of times. Mama and Daddy liked visiting with her, might near as much as I did.

I even opened the icebox and let her inspect the ice. Kalola's brown eyes sprang wide, then seemed to dance. The way she giggled and laughed when she first touched the frozen water reminded me of the little, excited, giggly laugh Betty used to have. Kalola was totally fascinated by the ice and asked question after question.

Most days we fished. Sometimes we used spears.

One time, as we headed for Kamaiki Point, Makalii pointed out the tall, red cliffs on the east side of Manele Bay. He told us that when his grandfather was a little boy, each island had its own chief. Then right before the 1800s, King Kamehameha decided he wanted to be king of all the Hawaii islands. When he and his army attacked Lanai, the warriors fought bravely. But Kamehameha had too many warriors and weapons he had gotten in trade from the haole.

"The warriors of Lanai chose not to die at the end of Kamehameha's spears," Makalii told us in a solemn voice. "They chose also not to be slaves. When the battle was lost, they leaped from the cliffs, there." He pointed. "They chose death on the rocks below and in the sea."

He told us that his grandfather and lots of the women and children had taken the canoes and sailed to Pu'uhonau 'O Honaunau—"the City of Refuge"— on the big island. A place of sanctuary, it was where sinners and war criminals would be forgiven. The women and children were considered prisoners of war and would be slaves of the Kamehameha warriors. But they reached the place and stayed for a while. When they returned, they were considered full citizens and not slaves or prisoners or anything.

Another time, as we fished off the coast not far

from Maui, the old man told us that he had only been to the City of Refuge once. It was when his wife was sick with the smallpox. He had taken her there, hoping the gods would forgive them for some unknown *kapu* or "sin" that they might have committed. Although the trade winds were favorable and the seas calm, they did not make it in time. She died, not long after they reached the city.

"But it was good," Makalii said. "At City of Refuge, all kapu are taken away. She is protected by the gods now. She safe and happy.

"Some day when I am old man, if get sick or ready to die—you take to the puuhonua at Honaunau."

Without thinking, both of us nodded.

Makalii smiled. "Promise?"

Both of us nodded again. It was a silly thing to ask us. Makalii wasn't old. Well, yeah he was, but he was strong and healthy. He'd live for a long, long time, so neither of us gave it much thought.

On Sundays, Kalola and I would not sit together in church. But afterwards, she would come by the house. The rest of the week, it was fishing or exploring or listening to Makalii and his fantastic stories of the gods or the old days.

In July, we had a really good fishing day. Just off Kaunolu Bay, we ran into a big school of ahi. When the three of us were done, Kalola's and my hands were raw and bleeding. Makalii was so tired, he could barely lift his last fish into the boat. The whole bottom of our outrigger was filled with fish. There was hardly any place to put our feet, and I had to dig to find my oar.

"Good catch," Makalii shook his head. "We take Keomuku."

It was almost dark when we reached the far side of the island. People came when they saw our boat. They waved and smiled and called out Makalii's and Kalola's names. But when they saw me, they stopped.

Makalii leaped out. I couldn't tell what he was saying because he spoke in Hawaiian. He kept stomping his foot and pounding his chest with a fist. The people stood around while he and two of the men talked and yelled, back and forth, for a long time. Finally, he motioned for Kalola and me to come.

With a big smile on his face and his chest puffed out proud, he put an old, callused hand on my shoulder and turned me to face the group of people.

"This not haole. This not John Priddle," he announced to the crowd. "This is my friend. This is Kioni. Pretty good fisherman. Come see our catch. Take what you need. Come see what Kioni, Makalii, and Kalola have for you."

It really made me proud that the old man felt that way about me.

I made a lot of new friends that evening. We ate and talked and some of the boys said they were going hunting for wild pig on Maui next week. They asked if I wanted to come along.

After we ate, there was a dance. Makalii told me it was

called the hula. A couple of dances, the men and women both did. In the first dance, the men stomped their feet and growled while the women swayed their hips from side to side. In the second, both the men and women made motions—pretty, smooth motions—with their hands. Kalola told me the hula told a story and if I watched the hands, I could tell what they were saying.

I couldn't.

The last dance was just for the women. Kalola joined them. She had on her bright, wraparound dress. And as she smiled and swayed and moved . . . well, she was different somehow.

Maybe just the way I saw her was different.

That night as we walked on the beach, we didn't talk like we usually did. We just walked. On our way back to the village and the fire and the noise and the people, I stopped.

I stood right in front of her and looked at her brown eyes in the moonlight. She smiled up at me. Then, stretching on her tiptoes, she kissed me.

Darned if I didn't kiss her back!

I'd never kissed a girl. It wasn't terrible—like I thought it would be. It didn't take my breath away or leave my head spinning or make me all quivery inside like the big guys at school had said.

It was just . . . well . . . it was kind of nice. Natural, like holding hands or something. Kalola was my best friend. Maybe that had something to do with it.

The thing that I *did* notice was that when we walked back to Keomuku, it was like I was in a dream and nothing was real. There were no people or huts or for that matter, no Lanai. It was just Kalola and Kioni.

   Like I said, that summer was the most wonderful time of my life.

When it ended, it nearly broke my heart.

Chapter 27

It was the last Saturday in August. Only one more Saturday before school was to start again. I got home early on account of a storm had whipped up, someplace far out at sea. The waves had started to roll in pretty good.

I think I would have been okay if I'd had my gingerroot. Only, that morning when I'd tried to rinse a fresh batch off in the pool, this yellow stuff was there. It got all over my hands and all over the gingerroot. I managed to get it off my hands when I washed them in the ocean, but the bark was still yellowish. Since Makalii didn't know what it was, I figured it best to be on the safe side and not use it until I asked Daddy if he knew what could have turned everything in the water all yellow.

Anyhow, without the gingerroot and the waves getting bigger and bigger, I'd asked Makalii to take me to shore.

Like I said, I got home kind of early. I was really surprised to hear Mama and Daddy talking when I stepped up on the porch. It was way too early for ei-

ther of them to be home from work. When I opened
the door, my mouth flopped open and my eyes might
near fell out of my head.

Mama and Daddy were in the living room. They
were packing our things.

"What—why?" I stammered.

"We're going back home," Mama announced.

"We're leaving Lanai!" Daddy said.

No amount of begging or pleading could change
their minds. I even cried. I hadn't done that since I
was a little kid, but the thought of leaving Lanai and
Kalola—I couldn't help myself.

I guess I had been having so much fun and enjoy-
ing myself so much, I'd never noticed how unhappy
Mama and Daddy were.

Seemed like Daddy had done everything under the
sun, other than falling on his knees and begging, to
get Paul Jacobs to buy chaps for the workers. Mr. Jacobs didn't seem to care if the men were all cut up or
not. Daddy had been working on a sprayer for the
pineapple fields. The pineapples needed potassium
and iron to grow, and though there was plenty of iron
in the red, rocky soil of Lanai, the pineapple roots
didn't pull it up. It had to be sprayed on the leaves.

Daddy had invented this sprayer thing that fit in
the back of a truck. An old, discarded car motor ran
the pump and long arms or pipes with holes in them
stuck out from either side. Daddy said that with the
sprayer, he could fertilize up to ten rows of pine-

apples from the back of the truck, instead of having the workers get all poked and cut up by walking down the rows with sprinkler cans.

Paul Jacobs said no.

"Why don't you wait until Mr. Dole gets back," I pleaded. "You said that Mr. Jacobs wasn't really your boss. Why don't you talk to Mr. Dole about it?"

Daddy shook his head.

"I'll not waste my time with a liar!"

I frowned and looked at Mama. She stuffed two more pairs of shoes into a burlap sack.

"Mr. Dole told us that he paid good wages and that no one—NO ONE—had to pay rent. It was a lie. Carmine had to go down to the docks this morning to send back a shipment of rotten bananas that came in. While she was gone, a woman dropped by to pay her rent. When I told her that she didn't have to pay rent and I didn't know what she was talking about, she went to the back room and made me look at the other set of books Carmine has. Sure enough—People are paying rent."

"Dole pays good wages," Daddy scoffed. "But every bit of it he gets back in high rent. The white people—us, the du Chances, Mr. Munro, Mr. Foster—our names aren't in the books. Just the kanakas. Just the Filipinos and Japanese—the workers who can't afford it."

"But won't you at least talk to him about it, Daddy. I mean, just . . ."

Daddy shook his head. "I'll not waste my time on a liar and someone as two-faced as James Dole or Paul

Jacobs. Mr. Dole is supposed to arrive tomorrow morning on his schooner. I'll stay around just long enough to tell him what I think of him. Then we're headed home!"

There was a finality about the way Daddy said, "headed home!" I realized that there was no changing his mind nor talking him out of it.

Reluctantly, slowly, I went to my room and started taking my shirts and pants off the hangers. Like dragging my feet through thick mud, I trudged to the living room and started packing stuff away.

Despite the fact that it took us three days to unpack, we packed everything up by that evening. Mama fed us sandwiches because she had already scrubbed the pots and pans and put them in the boxes Daddy and I built for the trip over here.

When I told them I had to go say good-bye to Makalii and Kalola, Mama and Daddy both told me they were sorry, but, "No!"

There was no answer when I called to the shack. I slipped down from Ginger's back and leaped to the porch. There was no door to knock on, so I stomped on the wood. Five times, as hard as I could.

"Kalola? Makalii?"

There was no answer. I shoved the blanket back and rushed inside. Even in the dark, I could tell the shack was empty. Still, I screamed their names again.

They couldn't be gone! They couldn't have gone out fishing again. Not as rough as the sea was.

I had to tell them what had happened. I had to tell them why I was leaving. I had to hold Kalola in my arms—one last time. I had to kiss her—one last time and tell her . . .

Ginger shied when I bolted from the house and raced toward the ocean. That's where I found them. When I called her name, I heard:

"Kioni. Here. Here at the boat."

I raced to her and she hugged me. I could hear the little whimpering sound that came from deep in her throat. I pried her loose and held her at arms' length.

In the light of the full moon, I could see the tears that streamed from her brown eyes and left glistening trails on her soft, bronze cheeks.

"What is it? What's wrong?"

She pointed to the boat.

"Makalii is very sick. He says he will die. He wants to go to the puuhonua. But I am not able to move the boat into the water." Her eyes welled up and another stream of tears raced down her face. "I've prayed to God, even prayed to Kane. Asked them to give me strength. God or Kane sent you."

Bawling again, she wrapped her arms around me and squeezed so tight it almost hurt. Dragging her with me, I shuffled to the outrigger. The old man lay near the bow. Both arms wrapped around his stomach, all he could do was moan. Moan, and every once in a while lift his head high enough to throw up in the tin bucket Kalola had put beside him.

"He needs a doctor," I whispered.

"I told him this," Kalola sniffed back her tears. "He

says doctors can't help. He says he is ready to die, but must reach puuhonua at Honaunau. Must die in City of Refuge. Must die with Kini, his wife. He won't listen to me. He made me promise. Now will you help me put boat in water?"

"I'm here," I soothed. "I'll help."

She buried her face against my chest.

"I will never see Kioni again," she sobbed. "I cannot hold sail and steer with paddle. I will never find big island in the dark." She lifted her head and tried to smile when she looked up at me. "But I want you to know . . . aloha."

It was somewhere between midnight and morning when I knew that, not just Makalii Pukui, but all of us were going to die.

"Out of the frying pan and into the fire." Grandma's words drummed in my ears in rhythm with the waves crashing against the outrigger. But this time it was more than "out of the frying pan . . ." This time it was much, much more. I knew—only I tried to keep chasing the thought out of my head. I knew that I was going to die.

I think I knew it the moment I helped Kalola shove the outrigger into the surf and jumped in. I think I knew it all along.

Chapter 28

It really surprised me to see the sunrise the next morning. By all rights, we should have been dead.

I mean, here we were, a sick man—unconscious in the bow of a little outrigger—me, holding the sail in the middle of the boat—something I wasn't very good at. And Kalola—a girl—in the back of the boat, steering with her paddle after she'd already told me she didn't know how to steer.

The waves were big. The moon set early so it was pitch dark. And to make matters worse, we had no water.

By all rights, we should have already been dead.

I don't remember deciding to go with them. I just did it.

Last night, I'd begged and pleaded with them to wait for me to get Mama and Daddy—to find someone, anyone, to help us. Makalii raised up on one elbow. Weak and feeble, he was still able to remind us of the promise we had made to take him to the City of Refuge on the big island. Home was far up the hill. It would take a long time to get my parents and bring them back. So I made Kalola wait with her grandfather while I ran after some gingerroot.

The water from the spring smelled real funny. It was a familiar odor, only I couldn't recognize it at the time. Anyway, I decided to wash the dirt off the roots with seawater. I found where Kalola had her school tablet, but I couldn't find any chalk. So I grabbed a piece of charcoal from the dead fire beside the hut.

NEED HELP

BIG ISLAND

CITY OF REFUGE

That's all I had time to leave scrawled on the slate tablet in the middle of the living room floor. It was fuzzy, and in the dark, I couldn't even tell if anyone could read it. Besides, with my luck probably no one would even find it.

After we paddled out beyond the breakers, I peeled the gingerroot with my pocketknife and washed the shavings off with seawater. Trouble was, the salt in the water really dried me out. But the sea was so rough and I was so busy with the sail, I didn't even have time to think about getting a drink.

Sometime after the moon went down, the sea seemed to calm a tiny bit. When I asked Kalola to hand me the water gourd from the back of the boat, I recognized the smell I'd noticed back at the spring.

"Creosote!" I managed to gasp, after all my gagging and spitting and coughing and sputtering.

"What is that word?" Kalola asked from the back of the outrigger.

I dropped the sail and began scooping handfuls of seawater into my mouth.

"Creosote," I repeated when I had as much of the oily, nasty stuff rinsed out of my mouth as I could. "It's an oil of some kind. I don't know how it's made or what it comes from, but we use it back in Oklahoma to soak fence posts. Keeps the moisture from rotting them and keeps the bugs out of the wood."

"It is bad?"

"I reckon. When I was little, I used to chew my fingernails. I remember, one time I was helping Daddy get some post out of this metal tank. I started to stick my finger in my mouth, and he slapped the tar outa my hand. Told me *never* to get my hands near my mouth when I was around the creosote."

"Will grandfather die?"

"I don't know," I answered her as truthfully as I could. "Depends on whether or not he drank much water or how much he mixed to make his poi. Depends on how much he got in him. From what I know of creosote, it ain't good."

I pulled the pole back up, held it between my feet, and watched as the wind caught and filled the cloth. We sailed on.

Sailed on into the dark night. Sailed farther and farther from the safety of our tiny island and into the huge, black emptiness of the Pacific.

* * *

It was indeed a surprise to see the sunrise that morning. Even more surprising was to see how close we were to the small, flat island.

"Kahoolawe," Kalola told me.

"Are there any towns there? Anywhere we might find a doctor?"

Kalola shook her head. "Not much water on Kahoolawe. Nothing there but a few goats and sheep. No town. No people. Fisherman sometimes stop to spend the night between islands. No one else."

We hugged the shore. Just about the time the channel between Maui and Kahoolawe opened up and we had to turn southeast to find the big island, I saw a man.

He stood on the sand, not far from a flock of goats and sheep. He had a beard and long hair. When I waved, he waved back.

I flipped the sail and spun our outrigger toward the beach. We slid up on the bank, not thirty feet from where he stood.

"Hey, Mister," I called. "Can you help us? Please?"

I told him about the old man and the creosote. I asked if he knew of anywhere we could find a doctor or get help.

"I tend sheep and goats," he motioned at the animals behind him. "But perhaps I can help."

He went to the boat and lifted the old man's head. Makalii smiled when he saw the kind face looking down at him. The man spoke, only I couldn't hear what he said. Then he took a gourd from his belt and held Makalii's head while the old man drank.

He handed me the gourd, and told me the water was for Kalola and me. Then he put three more gourds in the bottom of the boat. He said there was goat's milk in them. We were to make Makalii drink one, then fill it with salt water from the sea.

"If he will not drink the others, give him the seawater. It will make him thirst, so he will have to drink."

"Will he make it?" I asked.

"I cannot say."

With that, he helped us push the boat into the water. We just paddled a little ways, when I remembered I should have thanked him for the goat's milk and for his help and kindness.

Only when I turned around, he was busy moving his goats up the hill.

"Thank you!" I called as loud as I could.

Without turning, he waved and went on about his work.

We sailed all that day and into another night. The sea was much calmer. In the daylight, Kalola and I could see the clouds that clumped above the big island. We followed them until the moon went down. Then there was nothing but the dark.

Kalola and I took turns climbing to the front of the outrigger to hold Makalii's head and pour salt water or milk down him. By noon of the next day, we could see land.

I offered a little prayer of thanks, 'cause I never expected to see land—not ever again.

Near the coast, we turned right. Kalola had never been there. Our only guide was her memories of Makalii's stories. She knew we must pass a town, and she thought she could recognize the place when she saw it. We sailed down the coast of Hawaii. We passed the town of Kona. A bunch of fishing boats were harbored there. Once, we sailed close to a big steamer that was making its way out of port.

Makalii was still sick. He still said he wanted to die at the City of Refuge. But he seemed better. Now and then, he even sat up in the boat to throw up over the side. Along about dark, he sat up and pointed to the shore.

"The puuhonua!" he called, then slumped back to the bottom of the boat.

It took Kalola and me both to help him up the hill. His old, weak, frail, legs wouldn't hold him. We lifted and strained and staggered until we came to an enormous stone wall. The thing was a good six feet thick. Huge idols made of rock stood on immense stone platforms. There were no gates and once inside, we could see the ruins of old thatched huts.

We helped Makalii to the center of the place. There, he told us to leave him and go back to the boat. No matter how much we protested, he wouldn't listen.

"Please," he said. "If you love me, leave me here with Kane and Lono and Pele and my Kini. I must be alone with them."

Kalola and I fell asleep that night, wrapped in each other's arms.

Not once did I think of—a girl.

I just held her.

I held her tight, hoping—no, praying—that by holding her I could pull away some of her hurt. Somehow, some way, pull the sadness from her and take it right into myself. She was my world. All I wanted was to protect her. To keep her safe from harm and from pain.

Chapter 29

That's how Mama and Daddy found us the next morning—wrapped in each other's arms and asleep in the sand.

First off, I never expected anyone to find us 'cause I was pretty sure we were going to be lost forever in the ocean. Next, I figured if they ever did find the note I left, they'd be mad at me. I mean, not only did I run off in the middle of the night, but I set sail in the dark for some island I'd never been to—much less knew where it was or how to find it.

Mama and Daddy loved me. Maybe as much as I loved Kalola. They were just so happy to find us alive, they must have forgotten to be mad.

James Dole's private yacht bobbed up and down in the sheltered bay. I could see Captain Sanches and Ching Lung near the bow, watching us. Another man stood on the beach beside a small launch next to our outrigger.

We told Mama and Daddy about Makalii and the trip here. We explained the promise both of us had made to the old man about bringing him to this place. Then I stood very straight. With my shoulders back and my head high, I looked Mama and Daddy right in the eye.

"Kalola is alone," I said. "Now that her grandfather is gone, she has no one. I'm not leaving. I'm gonna stay here with her."

"Would rather go home."

The voice made all of us spin around. Makalii Pukui stood behind us. He leaned against a palm tree. His weak, feeble, old legs kind of trembled beneath him.

Kalola let out a gleeful little squeal and raced to him. I followed her. Mama and Daddy were hot on our heels.

Makalii rubbed his tummy with one hand and held his granddaughter for support with the other.

"Bitter seawater and sweet milk make old man tummy feel better. Maybe live after all. But throw up so much, make me feel empty. Got any food on boat?"

It was a wonder Makalii could even walk, what with all four of us clumped around him, trying to help. Slow and careful, we made our way toward the launch.

"We're not leaving," Daddy said as we walked. "Mr. Dole, there . . ." He motioned at the tall, slender man who stood between the outrigger and the launch. "Well, we had a long talk while we were trying to track you two down. He didn't know anything about charging the workers rent. We figure that was the Jacobses' doing. And . . . well . . . he likes my idea about the chaps to protect the workers' legs. He likes the motor-operated fertilizer sprayer I come up with, too."

Mr. Dole came to help when we reached the beach. I guess he heard what Daddy was saying.

"I'm in the pineapple business to make money." He took Mama's place under Makalii's arm and helped him walk. "I expect my people to work hard. In return, I pay good wages and give them a place to stay. Appears to me that Paul Jacobs was cheating the workers and me, both. We'll straighten things out. You can mark my word on that!"

Mama reached in the launch and moved the oar out of the way so that Makalii wouldn't trip over it when Daddy and Mr. Dole helped him in.

"We're staying, John. All of us. We're staying on Lanai."

I went to the boat and brought Daddy and Mr. Dole the gourd with the creosote in it. We pushed the launch off and James Dole worked the oars to get them back to the schooner. Kalola, Mama, and I followed them in the outrigger, which we tied on behind the schooner.

Captain Sanches sailed south, around the island. Ching Lung seemed to take great pleasure in visiting with Makalii and bringing him food from the galley. If the old man had eaten all Ching Lung brought, he would have exploded. We stopped at the port in Hilo and Captain Sanches went for a doctor.

Makalii ate like a little pig. He burped a bunch, but kept patting his stomach. "Tummy much better, now," he kept saying. The doctor at Hilo said he would be okay, but to keep giving him plenty of liquids and fruit for a week or so.

It was the very next afternoon when James Dole, Daddy, and José de los Santos had me show them where to park the car at Manele Bay and how to get to Makalii Pukui's home. Daddy and Mr. Dole had found three cans of yellow, powdered dye in the trunk of Paul Jacobs's car. On the drive down the hill, when they told me about it, I remembered how yellow the water was when I washed the ginger-root.

"I never could figure out why Paul Jacobs spent so much time pouring dye in the streams. Guess he was trying to find where the water was coming from that flowed into Mr. Pukui's spring."

"The whole Chrysler reeked of creosote," Mr. Dole added. "We found two full barrels of it and one empty barrel in the shed behind Paul Jacobs's house. He couldn't talk the old man into selling his land, and he couldn't scare him off with threats. I guess his last resort was to poison his water supply. What I can't figure out is why!"

"I've sent Captain Sanches for the sheriff, over on Maui," Mr. Dole informed Makalii, once we reached his home. "We're going to charge Paul Jacobs with attempted murder. Figure we can get him and his wife both on embezzlement, for stealing money from my workers. Just wanted to let you know. Anything else you want. You want to cuss him out or . . ."

"We'll hold him and you can beat him up," José broke in.

Makalii just smiled and shook his head.

"I will not hit."

I guess the whole bunch of us kind of jerked and gasped.

"But he tried to kill you," Mr. Dole insisted.

The old man just shrugged and took another bite of Mango. "Jacobs want whole island be Mr. Dole island. When I not sell, he try to run away by make water stink and make old man sick."

"I don't want the whole island," Mr. Dole protested. "I never did. I got more land now than I can possibly use. I never intended for . . ."

Makalii waved him to be quiet.

"I know this. Jacobs not know. Think he make akii happy . . ."

"*Akii* means 'boss,' " Kalola whispered to Mr. Dole.

". . . just make himself unhappy," Makalii went on. "He not very smart in head or very good in heart. But old man okay. Kalola and Kioni, okay. I forgive Jacobs. Not want in jail. Maybe just send away. That be okay with me."

Mr. Dole looked at Makalii for a long, long time. Finally, he sighed and shook his head.

"Don't think I ever met a man with a more Christian attitude. If that's all you want . . ."

"That all I want."

My mouth flopped so wide, a sea turtle could have walked in. I shook my head back and forth hard enough to make my brain rattle. But, before I could protest or say anything, Daddy nudged me with an elbow. He leaned over and whispered:

"Remember that special kind of love he talked about?" That's all Daddy said.

Don't reckon he needed to say anything else.

Things were a lot different on Lanai, once the Jacobs family left. James Dole tried to make Daddy the foreman of the whole pineapple plantation. Daddy didn't want any part of it, so he suggested José de los Santos. He told Mr. Dole that José knew more about pineapples than anyone on the island. Besides, Daddy liked inventing and tinkering with stuff.

Mr. Dole agreed.

Mr. Foster left not long after the Jacobs. Miss Blevins, our new teacher, made school a lot more fun. She was every bit as strict as Mr. Foster, but she was nice. All of us sat together and she treated us all the same. After the first couple of weeks, Robert and the rest of the guys even started including me in their baseball games.

Makalii finally got the creosote out of his taro patch. He was happy.

Mama ran the Mercantile. She treated everybody decent and nice. Daddy tinkered and messed with stuff. He remembered the conveyor belts at the pineapple plant in Honolulu and decided to rig something like that on the back of the pineapple trucks to help with the harvesting.

At school, Kalola and I didn't sit together. After school, we went our separate ways and met at Mr. Munro's pen for the ride home on Ginger.

Reckon both of us can hardly wait till next summer.

Aloha.